The Marrakech Express

The Marrakech Express

Carlotta Ladyizumi Abrams

LiFi Publications Pvt. Ltd.
New Delhi

Published by:
LiFi Publications Pvt. Ltd.
211, 2nd Floor, Gagandeep
12, Rajendra Place, New Delhi–110 008, India
Phone : (011) 2574 1000
E-mail : info@lifipublications.com
Web : www.lifipublications.com

ISBN: 978-93-86191-95-3 (PBK)
ISBN: 978-93-86191-96-0 (HBD)

First published in 2019

Cataloging in Publication Data—DK
[Courtesy: D.K. Agencies (P) Ltd. <docinfo@dkagencies.com>]

Abrams, Carlotta Ladyizumi, 1966– **author.**
The Marrakech Express / Carlotta Ladyizumi Abrams.
pages cm
Novel.
ISBN 9789386191953 (PBK)
ISBN 9789386191960 (HBD)

1. American fiction. I. Title.

LCC PS3603.B73M37 2019 | DDC 813.6 23

Printed in India by D.K. Fine Art Press (P) Ltd., Delhi–52

To Hiram 'Hiroo' Theodore Kato

Acknowledgements

I wish to thank my late mother Mariko Takahashi Abrams, for her tireless love and sacrifice. I also want to express appreciation to my high school friend, Rachael Apanovitch for her support. I thank Anne Greene, Director of Writing Programs at Wesleyan University, for starting my path and professors R. Lincoln Keiser and David Adams for believing in me. I also thank the Blackwell family, for the music. I am indebted to my Wesleyan friends Ed Boyden, Debra Isserlis Steppel, Jeffrey Needelman, Josef Astienza, and Mary Gelezunas for understanding class issues and being there for me. For the times in San Francisco and Berkeley, I thank Moonsong and Mary Oakley and Katherine 'Kippy' Isham Phelps. I thank Jeanne Moulton Cashman, John Maddigan for the times in Amherst. This project would not have been possible without the constant support of my always there friend, the late Hiram Kato. My writing teachers at Arizona State University, Ron Carlson, William Kittredge, and Beckian Goldberg were instrumental in supporting my path. Special thanks to the late poet Ai. My PhD advisor at the University of Southern Mississippi, Sandra Shattuck, helped me to believe in my writing. Thanks as well to fellow writers and scholars for our workshops in Hattiesburg – Charlie Braxton and Johnnie Robinson, and Sister in the Struggle, Dr. Teresa Washington. I appreciate crew – Ralph Peralta, Valerie Rochon, Tony Gonzalez, Larry Callahan, Ricky Sanchez, Misty LaSalvia, Matt and Sue Roe, Cheryl Lehman and Bridget Murphy.

My Asian colleagues and family have helped me straddle cultures: appreciation goes out to my Takahashi family members and members of ASIAPAC conferences including my mentor, Edwin Thumboo and Dr. FaridahManaf as well as Kirpal Singh. For helping me in Oregon, I appreciate Dan Jones, Thomas Alberti, and the late Dennis Hey. Further appreciation goes out to Dr. Lisa Sjodin-Feldman, the Selby family and James Melki. This work would not be possible without the tireless work of my editors, H. Lee Barnes and Mary Sojourner, who believed in me. I appreciate A J Thomas for his love of my work and his connecting me to LiFi Publications. I want to thank Captain Arul Anantham and his sister Daisy for their caring and hospitality. To Fiend, the rapper, I appreciate the food, music, and love. Lastly, my love goes out to Robert Paine Cummings and Maya, forever and for always.

1

In 1986, the world was full of the last breaths of life and hope for the 1960's and Lumita Cleopatra Sugarman bought it. She was born at the end of the 60's whose iconic images carried her through to her life at Middlesex, a private Connecticut college. She read Buddhism, she continued her tutoring program at the Apple Lane detention facility and she waited for her boyfriend Bob to visit her from San Francisco. Bob was a long haired activist whom Cleo had met the summer before while working on the bottle redemption bill at CALFORCE. Bob had protested through the tear gas of the 60s and early 70s and had even seen Jimi Hendrix and the Doors. Bob, however, was 3000 miles away and Cleo's progressive college was full of fake activists from Bethesda and Manhattan. She listened to the strains of their activist meetings and they looked beyond her. But the game was always on at the fraternity house and Cleo, who had grown up with three brothers, liked to watch the fights and the games.

Duane, the captain of Middlesex's lacrosse team, kept calling and in her brown and orange tinged loneliness, Cleo would have dinner and visit the short, compact fraternity member in his 'In Town' apartment. When she met Bob, she had stopped talking to Duane, but kept running into him when she was studying in the two Middlesex libraries. The stately buildings of Middlesex could not hide their financial aid students; it was as if they were exposed in klieg light in their plush study chairs. The students called Duane's housing unit 'Tin Town,' as the walls were so thin that you could hear everything. Some nights, she ran out of Tin Town, her mouth tasting of cheap champagne and compromise.

Cleo's tutoring program was going well. The new experiences came so quickly then, that she had little time to analyze them. She was trying to experience everything to the fullest. Cleo, who already had long black hair, began wearing thrift store army pants and jackets and listened intently to Professor David Davison discussing the 'Consciousness Development of Peace Activists'. She read about Mandela, union leaders, and movements for change. She took a course of 'Women's Health' and learned about the Boston Women's Health Collective. Cleo was relieved to have a female professor. Leaving the fraternity house and the WEDU heavy metal show, she was surrounded by men with whom she shared sports and music, but not much else. The Health class was full of lectures on the clitoris, the dangers of the pill, and how technology controlled the female body. She talked to Bob on the payphone about this, and he agreed with the professor. But Cleo needed more than an agreeable, progressive voice on the phone.

Bob kept saying that he was going to visit. He was living in a converted gardening shed in San Francisco, however, and Cleo knew he needed every weekly paycheck to get by. Ed Boykin, Cleo's friend who wore combat boots and lumberjack shirts, answered Bob's calls on the payphone. When Cleo took the phone from Ed, the two were talking about Noam Chomsky. Cleo told Bob that Frank, who had worked for CALFORCE with them in Santa Cruz, had already moved to Amherst, as promised, and was now working at MASSFORCE. Frank had seen 500 Grateful Dead concerts and all of his belonging fit in a backpack. Cleo heard Bob sigh all the way from the Avenue Club, where he worked as a bartender for a second job.

Finally, on one spring day of the year that the Internet Engineering Task Force was meeting in California, Bob appeared on the green lawns of the campus. The trees were bursting with leaves and flowers. Bob's long hair flowed down onto his leather jacket and he wore his flare-legged corduroy jeans. Cleo hugged him, laughing as one of Middlesex's athletic teams jogged by. Cleo immediately took Bob over to the room, which was located within view of some oak trees and past the big hill near the huge observatory.

"I need some help, that drug dealer next door has been making fun of my late night studying and my ramen noodles," she said.

"I got it," Bob said. He put down his army bag and walked next door. When Cleo returned from the bathroom, she saw that the student looked ashen, as if he had been in front of a judge after committing a crime. His face looked resembled that of a weasel, going back into his hole. She walked through the dorm and looked into her friend's rooms.

"He's here," she said, calling into rooms full of decorations from Heavy Metal posters to Disney motifs. Cleo also called Evan and Harold, from the WEDU heavy metal show, the Witching Hour. Even Niema, Harold's sister came by. She was teetering on heels, and brought a bottle of gin from the corner 'packie'. Her coffee skin reflected in the bottle as she handed it to Bob, holding him in a hug. Bob was exhausted, but as Cleo held him on her tiny bed, she could hear the strains of Jefferson Airplane and the faint strains of Ed talking about Christopher Hitchens. Her roommate, Mary Gemelunas then put Fairport Convention on her record player. Mary had her rolls of fabric for costumes lying around her and she was smiling. It was as if ancient Eastern Europe was right there in the dorm. Debbie Stepman, down the hall, knocked on the door. She was from Bellows Falls, Massachusetts. Her father had owned a party goods/paper company. 'Little Debbie' as they called her, often participated in the chorus and she also worked on many social awareness issues at Middlesex. She brought a welcome card and a dish to share.

Bob and Cleo shared the bed and let the rays of New England morning sun wake them. Mary was off to her Russian literature class.

Bob got up, ran to the bathroom, and back to her room. He brushed his hair with his silver monogrammed brush and scooped up her books. Cleo got into her army jacket and jeans and followed as he carried her books to class across the green lawns and past the early nineteenth century buildings of Middlesex. As she walked, she read from an article on the history of French colonialism in Morocco, and Rob translated the French phrases for her. In class, she translated them and smiled. Cleo recalled her father saying that she had distant ancestry from the region. She let the lyrics slip off her tongue:

'Looking at the World
Through the Sunset in your eyes
Trying to make the train
Through clear Moroccan skies…
Would you know we're riding
On the Marrakech Express
All onboard that train…'

Bob had to leave for Boston, to visit his mother and his brother. She saw him off at the Trailways bus on the part of the town by the river, and hunched her shoulders to walk up the hill.

Cleo's tutoring program had gotten her some attention. She had been hired as a tutor coordinator and a tutor by Peter Budkin, who ran the Upward Program at Middlesex. Her mixed race, part Japanese, but with undistinguishable features, gave her credibility with the local high school students from low income and minority backgrounds. When they asked her where her family was from, she would say 'from all over, from the atlas to the desert, where colored cottons hang in the air'. Having grown up forty minutes away in North Mills, which the students thought of as 'Appalachia', Cleo could talk the talk of TV and trucks. Cleo was allowed to drive the white Econovan to the Meriden location, where she would bring students from Middlesex to tutor the Upward students. Budkin was conservative, so Cleo had to try to 'play the part'. He was a bit older than her professors or Bob, and seemed to have no alternative culture leanings. Like Mr. Washing, her Middle School English teacher, he was into fly fishing. Cleo wondered how many people spent time in high boots throwing lines in the water, when they could simply go to the grocery store. When Bob was there, Cleo had avoided Budkin's office, which was in the lower section of campus.

"Are you going to the lacrosse game?" Budkin asked, looking over his book, his gray hair the same color of his book. "Duane is the star, AND he is going to work for ME this summer." Cleo looked down.

"I am busy this weekend, my boyfriend is visiting," Cleo said, rushing down the wooden steps. She was working as a secretary at the Liberal Studies office and at Upward Bound. She also tutored delinquents. She worried, that, like those long lines in water, she would be caught up in her own evasions of the different stories and ways of being.

Bob was scheduled to stay for three weeks before returning back to San Francisco. He was taking the Trailways down to Middlesex and Cleo had been up for 24-hours, studying and working. Cleo was done taking a shower, and Mary Gemelunas came back to the room. She stared at Cleo, her eyes wild. Her handmade purple dress was flowing around her goddess body.

"I can't believe it," she said. "I put this song on the record player, then I went out onto Foster Hill, and there he was, playing it on a guitar. It was Phil Ochs's song, *Changes*. He could not have heard that I was playing it; he's psychic," she added. Bob had borrowed heavy metal musician Evans' guitar and was playing tunes on the hill, *Sit by my side, come as close as the air, share in a memory of gray; Wander in my words, dream about the pictures that I play of changes*. Phil Ochs had committed suicide, but Cleo did not think of it at that moment. The grass was beautiful and the tunes soft. Bob's visit to Middlesex brought a light to the hill that Cleo had never seen.

On Friday, Bob and Cleo boarded the Trailways up to Boston. Bob told Cleo that he had gone to see his mother, but he had not seen her yet. Cleo looked at Bob as the bus chugged up Interstate 84. Places Cleo had spent teen years at like the Enfield Mall, the Holyoke Mall, The Eastern States Exposition, and the Springfield bus station seemed old, relics of the 1970s. She thought of the people she had known and being with a 'hippie' on the bus seemed to elevate her off the asphalt of the freeway and up into the New England where Bob was raised.

As the bus pulled into Newton for a stop, Bob said, "just wait for me after I come from the train this evening. Look, there is Weston, where I went to the Cambridge School. I will tell you about it some time." The bus pulled into Boston, and Bob looked around, laughing. Cleo took his hand as they headed for the underground 'T'. They took the Green Line, lurching under Boston into Cambridge. As they exited the station into Harvard Yard, Bob smiled, "I wonder if Jack's is still open?" he said. They walked the cobblestone streets, stopping in Leo's Place, with its old clientele and the red 50's era booths. Bob ordered a Miller for them and started to talk to the old man next to him about the Red Sox. The smell of Leo's Place was like Thanksgiving for Bob and Cleo, a place where two sides met and talked over beer and snacks. They went out of Leo's to see what used to be Claire Lemoyne's big white house, right on Brattle Street. Bob's high school girlfriend was now living in Vermont, baking breads. The house seemed to own the street. The people walking by dared not tread on the small lawn and brick that led to the front door. Bob went to the corner and ordered a sandwich. It was not just any sandwich; it was an Elsie's roast beef sandwich. The sandwiches filled their hands and dripped down their fingers. In the 1980s, a few townies and old WASPs could still be seen strolling in the streets. Bob had his corduroy blazer on and Cleo felt like he was 'holding court'. She knew that Budkin would not belong here. Cleo waited at a coffee shop while Bob took the Blue Line to the Wonderland racetrack, where his mother's companion would pick him up and take him to Marblehead. Cleo was half way through the Marx and Engels Reader, hopped up on strong coffee, when Bob arrived, his eyes glassy and his tone of voice low. They did not talk much, but headed to the Peter Pan station, where they waited till 5 a.m. on the plastic seats. Cleo lay on his shoulder, listening to his Marlboro effected breathing. They held hands as the bus left Boston and swung into the green interior of Massachusetts, past farms and candle shops and old gas stations.

Cleo had not been in New England with someone who was part of its fabric this way. Her father was the loose end of a badly hooked rug, with no center. She did not know the stitches that made him and had not met the people who were part of the coloring of the floor piece. Cleo's mother did not seem to belong to these Northern states. Cleo was admitted to Middlesex, but resented its privileged students. Bob seemed to know codes and rules that she might never know. The Amherst green, with its benches and Lord Jeffrey Inn, where the UMASS student Andrew Valerian had taken her for a drink in high school, never seemed to change physically. They walked off the bus, which stopped at the stationary store and Bob guided her through the cafes and bars of the town where he had spent time while at Hampshire College. They took the PVTA to Northampton, where Bob got himself a room at an SRO, the Bay State Hotel, right next to the Pearl Street Music club. The old buildings seemed to breathe smoke and blues while life whittled down to a small room and a bottle. Bob was happy to note that the Bay State was still open, with the same bespectacled old man at the desk. Cleo peeped in to see the old, bald man reading the paper behind a 1950's style desk. She could see a staircase behind the desk and the smell of urine and smoke came from above. It was an SRO, so Cleo was not allowed to stay with Bob. The next weekend, however, Cleo learned to scramble up the fire escape and crawl into the tiny bed with Bob.

That week, Cleo glowed in her classes. The students asked about Bob, who had sat in on her professor's classes; Coop, or Cooper's anthropology and Davidson's psychology. The professors and students had stared at Bob and tried to concentrate. Bob just listened, and watched as Cleo commented, with a new sense of self-esteem, about her scholarship. Bob stayed in the Pioneer Valley at the SRO that week, though, and was scheduled to return to San Francisco after that.

"I'm not going back," his voice on the phone resonated. Bob said that he had got a job at Mass Share, an economic justice group, and all he needed was in his backpack. After all, he said, "all that I need is here with me." Cleo could hear the sound of more coins being inserted into the payphone. She had so many new responsibilities – the tutoring programs, advanced classes, law school applications coming up, and now this.

"We can talk when I see you again," he said, "We don't have to be exclusive, you are so young, you can date if you like, but you know how I feel."

"I do, Bob, I love you." She said, "Date, heehee, that's a funny word," Cleo said. "You know Peter Budkin got me that internship in DC this summer. But it's paid, so you can come see me and I can see you."

This was yet another layer. Cleo would be in a new city on a huge grant, the Middlesex Scholar Program. Budkin had put in the application behind her back when she told him that she might be in San Francisco that summer.

2

"Your friend Duane is working for me now," Budkin said as Cleo walked into the office. "He's really athletic and he will run our Outward program for high school students." Cleo gasped.

"You will be in DC on that grant, and he will be here, but I am sure he will visit," Budkin said. "Where were you these weekends? I thought you were home in Westchester," he said, lightly laughing. The new tutor Joe walked in and saved Cleo.

"Hi Lumita, are we going to Meriden today?" Joe asked. Joe had been 'abandoned' by a Cuban father and was raised by a Basque American mother in the City. He was gay and shared Cleo's 'outsider' status.

"Remember, you are going to fly to DC for that conference next weekend," Budkin called to Cleo's back. 'I am not from Westchester,' Cleo thought, and he knows it.

3

This city was no New York or San Francisco. It was the South. The organization was run by Dr. Clovis Mitchell, or Mitch, who has a leg affected by polio, and a curriculum vita and list of friends that included Kennedys and many Senators. He had spent years lobbying Congress and Senate to fund education. Maureen Heinemann had attended law school at Georgetown when Mitch was there. They were a powerful professional pair, and it would be an interesting summer. People from the West Indies staffed the office, and the flavor of DC at the time was deep and soulful, if a bit dangerous. Dupont Circle was populated by drug addicts, not gourmet cafes. The organization was lobbying, in tough times, for poor students.

That spring visit, Cleo went up to Capitol Hill. Dressed in one of her three professional dresses, Cleo walked with a woman who wore a peach colored skirt with low heels and an accent from an island. She looked up to see the many, many steps. Cleo thought of how her great grandfather had fought to keep these steps to the top, to keep the woman next to her from being in shackles and to allow her mother to come across an ocean. The walk seemed endless, but they finally reached their destination. They entered through security without badges, as if they were known. They went to several offices to deliver packages, low heels clicking on slick floors. The secretaries and the people in the inner offices all smiled at them.

"We've got two more," the woman said. They went down the steps and off to another office building, up an elevator and into a big office suite. The name said, Thomas P. 'Tip' O'Neill. Cleo's eyes opened wide.

"Sorry, it was just St. Patrick's Day, the Speaker is out," the woman behind the desk smiled. The woman in peach smiled knowingly and handed her the package.

"We know you are with us," she said and made small talk for a bit. Cleo stared at the walls, the pictures and the awards. She thought of that shock of white hair and the booming voice.

Mitch had sent his regards to O'Neill. The elevators were full of power suits and the smell of sex. They then went out and tried Ted Kennedy's office. He was not in that day either. Cleo never imagined that these offices would someday be emptied of their pictures and awards. Like Bob, they seemed timeless.

4

The word 'Intern' has been besmirched by scandal, but DC lived up to its reputation for wild times, political intrigue, and steamy days and nights. As Cleo sat in the well appointed kitchen signing the short-term lease, dressed in her pink oxford, Mrs. Lindemore said, "I want you to know that Tom Brokaw still keeps his house here. We are neighbors." Cleo handed her a cheque from her new chequebook. A few weeks later, she saw the same man that interviewed Gorbachev, Putin, and Reagan, taking out the trash. She wondered if Roger Mudd, who her father had watched for years, was in there. But that day, she went downstairs into the dank room, for which she paid $300 monthly and tacked up a T-shirt with a peace sign.

The bus that went from the posh neighborhood through into DC showed a slice of America. It was a gritty city, the homeless and drunks out in force. The crime statistics from DC in 1986 show that there were almost two hundred murders, and this number would double in the next few years. Cleo could feel the breath of centuries in the tiny corner marts and on the late night buses, using skills Bob had taught her to avoid conflict. They had stayed in Oceanview in San Francisco, where they had to avoid late night gangs of youth. But DC was entirely different. The Educational Association was busy, and Cleo was compiling a list of all the programs across the US. Cleo called from Guam to Puerto Rico, talking to directors and compiling information for the government. The office was always hosting directors and politicians, and the office workers from the Islands and Cleo were busy shuttling them around, working on the list of programs, and going up to the Hill.

5

Pete Seeger sang *This Land Is Your Land*, the song that Cleopatra's mother sang to her as a child. The celebrities and folk singers were out getting exposure on the weekend of the big protest. The same city that had surged with slaves and colonists, the same city that Cleo had shuffled through as a naïve eighth grader with leering teachers, was the home of a conservative government that had the kind of power that controlled the people in the tobacco fields Cleo had worked in as a youth. She was mad as hell. The mall was thronged by thousands of people – labor activists with union signs, aging hippies, college students, and people of color. The surge of people moved as a body, chanting in English and Spanish. Signs protested 'Bush's Dirty War'. Cleo imagined that people in North Mills were going to soccer games, swimming in the town pond, or maybe shopping at the Enfield Mall. She was standing where King had given his famous speech. She felt her voice chanting with these protestors against the government policies. As Cleo chanted '*Si se puede*' she felt as if she finally belonged in this country. This was a country that had caused her immigrant mother and Cleo great pain, but it was also a country that still allowed voices to chant in the street. The people chanted, hoping that Reagan, the actor, could hear them. Cleo saw stilt puppets and people with masks. She saw pictures of the dying in El Salvador and Guatemala, funded by US tax dollars. She raised her fist as Bob had years ago, and watched as cameras recorded her. She waved her hand at them. Cleo noticed a thin man with a yellow flag.

"Excuse me, Sir, how much farther will we be marching?" she asked.

"About a mile," the Peacekeeper told her. He had long, sandy hair tied in a ponytail and a bit of an accent. They walked and chanted together. Finally, they sat down on the grass to listen to speeches.

"I'm Bobby Lee Purcell," he said, extending his hand. "I am the son of a Vietnam veteran and the grandson of the long-time Mayor of Bazoo, Mississippi, Charles Loomis 'Dusty' Purcell. I am here because I am trying to right the wrongs my family did."

"I am Lumita Cleopatra Izumi Sugarman," Cleo said, "You can call me Cleo. I am here to bear witness for the oppressed." Bobby had spent summers on Dusty's plantation, as his father went to various military stations. Dusty fired a sanitation worker during the Civil Rights era, because the worker went to an organizing meeting. Fannie Lou Hamer had worked on a plantation nearby. Cleo listened, intrigued.

"Why don't you come and meet some other protesters," Bobby said. After the speeches wrapped up, Bobby took Cleo through the DC streets.

"I need to use the bathroom," Cleo said.

"No problem," Bobby said. They stopped in front of a hotel. Bobby whispered to the doorman, who was dressed in a gold trimmed red outfit. He let them in to the interior of the Hay Adams hotel, where Cleo walked past men in suits and women with shoulder pads and high heels. The bathroom was bigger than most of the living rooms she knew. She quickly did her business. Cleo was wearing a tie-dyed T-shirt and army pants. The woman standing next to her at the sink stared at her. Cleo quickly rushed out of the Hay Adams. Bobby was waiting outside. They walked past hotels and cafes and out towards Lafayette Park and around to the front of the White House.

"Charles, this is Cleo, Cleo this is Charles," Bobby said. Cleo met Dr. Charles Hyder, ex-NASA astrogeophysicist, who was fasting for peace in front of the White House. Hyder had a ragged beard, a tent, a sleeping bag, and books and articles about nuclear war. Cleo looked across the street at the White House, with its columns and lamp hanging from a chain and wondered what Ronald Reagan was doing in there. Hyder took out his articles and books and began to talk about the destruction of the planet. Bobby sat down, and Cleo sat down next to him.

After they met Charles, Bobby introduced Cleo to Conception Picciotto, who sat with her pictures of Hiroshima and Nagasaki. Cleo looked at these people who were seated on the ground and wondered how long they could continue this. The bored security guards at the White House glanced occasionally at the protesters, talking to each other and pointing. The air was thick and slightly sweet, wetter even than the air in the fields Cleo had worked in. As it grew dark, Cleo felt the clenching of the streets, as if they were no longer in America, as if the donkey carts and women with baskets on their heads would appear soon.

After going to her work at the association, Cleo spent many nights with these people, talking about physics, Hiroshima, hope for peace, and the need for political change. Bobby and she went back to his apartment in Adams Morgan, then a middle class area with many immigrants. They dropped off fruits and melons for the drug addicts in Dupont Circle. People pushed shopping carts around and Cleo saw men sticking needles into pulsing veins and then discarding them into a fountain. People with smudged faces and tattered clothes plunged into the melons, their faces full of red, yellow, or orange.

After work one Friday, Cleo took off her button down, exposing the tie-dye underneath. She took the bus to Adams Morgan, sweating in the 99-degree heat. She walked to the brick house and down the steps into the basement. Bobby opened the screen door. The heat escaped the room. He gestured to her and she sat down on the sofa. The metal springs poked at her. They sat next to each other in the heat, reading the Bible and the works of Mennonite activists. Someone had just tried to snatch Cleo's purse. They read about 'Compassion.' Bobby reached over and put his hand under Cleo's tie-dye.

Two days later, Cleo was walking down the K Street. The dusk was settling over the city, the brownstone lights lit up all over the town. Packages passed from hand to hand and couples linked in hotels and on park benches. Nearby, The Potomac seethed with dead bodies, military trainees, and secrets. Cleo's arm jerked. Someone pulled at her loose knit bag. Cleo felt the furor of all that she had experienced: the tobacco boss leering, garbage clean up, her brother's blows, racial taunts, freezing on the ground and watching popular girls in high school. Cleo's whole being rose up from the swamp and she pushed with all that was in her brown/yellow skin.

"You won't take it, you won't take me," she screamed. She pushed and grabbed what was hers. She threw the man down as if she were one of the wrestlers depicted on ancient urns. Cleo was ancient. She was part of her mom, but not her mom. The man tumbled down and rolled. She grabbed her bag and ran. She ran towards the White House. Despite the dangers on the street, Bobby and Cleo still went to Lafayette Park until late. They used the bathroom at the exclusive Hay Adams hotel. Cleo looked out from the lobby windows into the steaming summer heat, exiting always into protests, Capitol Hill, and the cobbled change she felt.

6

The first time Cleo saw crack was in DC. The city was moving around like the Central American wars that the country was in. All kinds of merchants, spies, soldiers, politicians in suits and laborers filled the sweaty streets with their frenetic pace. The buses were white, striped with a little blue and red. On one steamy Saturday evening in late June, Bobby and Cleo got off one of those buses and walked to his basement apartment. Bobby sat down on the couch and opened the Bible while Cleo rummaged through the fridge. Her eyes focused on a glass pipe sitting in the shelf in the door. Bobby's roommate Don, who wore a big moustache and a white under shirt, reached behind her. He worked with Bobby on construction sites, and talked about politics, but Don was in a general haze. He was pleasant, but had an edge. He grabbed his pipe.

"That's crack," Don said, "It's new on the scene." Don was a thin guy, with laborer's muscles. He leaned out and held it in the air, "Want some?"

"No, I have even stopped drinking for a while," Cleo said. "Bobby and I are learning about how coke is getting to the US from the CIA." Don shrugged, took the pipe, and went into his room. Bobby closed the Bible and moved Cleo's hand toward his crotch. Bob always had a softer way of touching, which took time and felt every bit of Cleo's mixed self. Duane went in like a lacrosse player, quick and tough. Bobby was somewhere in between.

Bobby and Cleo ate at African restaurants and saw a movie or two or went to a protest, but they did not go to bars or concerts. Cleo saw vials on the street. Police cars with flashing lights were everywhere.

Most interns of that time period stayed close to the Northwest part of DC, but Bobby and Cleo travelled all over the city, mingling with people. Some DC residents wore a popular hat from the time: 'Poor but Proud'. They went into convenience stores at midnight, getting items for the Vigil. The trees on the sidewalks seemed choked by the air, as if they would not last much longer. Cleo and Bobby walked at dusk in Rock Creek Park, where intern Chandra Levy's body would be found decades later. This was not the kind of nature Cleo wanted. When Cleo was away from Bobby, she called Bob from payphones.

The crack pipe, to her, was the image of a new era. The hippies were gone. Bobby, who was younger than the hippies and harsher, said, "Someday, the hippies will be in museum exhibits." Cleo knew that no real hippie would pick that tiny pipe up. About the same week Cleo saw the pipe, Duane sent her a letter on Bear Stearns stationary. After Outward Bound, Duane was interning at the investment company in New York City. The letter was optimistic, about Wall Street meetings and luncheons. All of this swirled in Cleo's head – Wall Street, the Central American war, crack, peace protests, and Capitol Hill. She longed for the trees.

7

The Amtrak chugged out of DC. Cleo was listening to her walkman and her backpack was full of books on politics and beatnik poetry. She could see the light over the grit. The train left the tough city and moved up through green corridors where secret things happened, things that Cleo protested. These suburbs were leafy, and one could imagine spies dropping packages in the blue postboxes on corners. The night on the train was comforting, the rhythm of going to home, although it was not a place, but a person. She heard the sound of the crossings and the whistles and the lonely towns as she passed through. She would soon see many cities and towns at night, crossings and bicycles, motorcycles, people, young and old waiting for the carriages to pass. The train started to slow as it eased into what would soon become Cleo's hub, a City where Jean Michel Basquiat was creating his art. Cleo could see the graffiti, even at night, the way it was in the 80s, claiming home and turf. She could almost hear the distant sounds of jazz, some salsa and meringue, and, yes, some rap emerging out of the gullet of the late night. Cleo emerged from Grand Central, where 'crack heads' emerged from the shadows. Grand Central was open all night, with no jackbooted Homeland Security types doing a 3 a.m. sweep. Cleo walked all the way to the Port Authority, not as familiar with the subway as she should have been. She had an army backpack and a jean jacket. Her jeans had the graffiti from the fields, and she had let her hair go wild. She was tan from the protests. She looked like she had nothing. She didn't.

4 a.m. at the Port Authority. Transvestites walked about, not the smiling ones seen on those respectable shows. These transvestites had

6-inch heels and huge breasts and were hollering towards the ceiling. Junkies twitched and gang members signaled signs that Cleo thought she might know from the fields. People were throwing up, and there was no one to clean it. It smelled like piss. In the 1980s, a lot of NYC had the smell of piss that had not been cleaned for years. Tricks and Johns and baby mamas all called out in various accents and colors to the homeland, which no longer existed, except on these streets. They were going to DC, Carolina, Buffalo, Boston, Miami – they were going or staying, hookin' and praying to a God that once looked over a city that was breakin' and rapping and muraling at a fevered pace. This was pre-Giuliani New York. The girl in hippie clothes drunk it all in, talked to people and watched a few cops throw down a few people on the floor, blood oozing from knees and noses. When the Springfield bus pulled in, Cleo was not on crack, but she might as well have been, as she was dazed, ready for the love of a man who enjoyed jazz and reading aloud to her at night. When she saw him at the Peter Pan Station in Northampton, she ran to him.

"Come with me to the Grateful Dead/Bob Dylan concert at RFK stadium," Cleo said.

"I have not been there since the 1960s, when I interned at the Post," he said, laughing, "but I will consider it." They walked in the college town, stopping at a café, where the strains of folk music played to them. That music clashed with the New York and DC sound, but it calmed Cleo, like Joan Baez talking to Jimi Hendrix. Cleo stayed with Bob at a room near Hampshire College, hitchhiking out of town to put their feet in the streams of the Pioneer Valley. They walked in the rolling New England hills until the summer sunset brought them to see the soft music.

8

The Grateful Dead and Bob Dylan concert was scheduled on the July 4th weekend. Bob agreed to come down to DC, even though he knew that the city represented a lot of the things that he despised. Cleo took the bus from her 'exclusive' neighborhood, through the teeming city, and over to the Greyhound station. The station was in the depths of the District, with its 'crack heads' and homeless. Bob got off the bus with his small army pack. He looked around at the urban milieu and said, "I need a drink." Cleo took Bob to Whitlows, right next door. Bob downed a Bacardi and looked around at the old timers and the travelers and the lifers.

"It aint the Haight," he exclaimed.

"Let's go," Cleo said. They took the red, white and blue buses to the Northwest. It was a weekend and the Lindemore's were home. Perhaps even Tom Brokaw was in town. As Bob and Cleo were going down the stairs, Mrs. Lindemore was taking the laundry up. She blanched and a pastel pair of cropped golf pants and polo fell on the stairs. The son, wearing a Georgetown T-shirt, peeked from above with a smirk on his face. Immediately, Cleo grabbed Bob's bag and put it on the floor. She opened the basement door into the light and headed out.

"Ah, Georgetown, I know it well," Bob said.

"Well, let's go there," Cleo mumbled. They walked to the bus stop and took the first bus to the heart of DC's elite. They walked the cobbled streets and stopped at a bar with old lamps lit outside. Bob opened the wooden door and took Cleo into the dark interior. The wood smelled as if it had been there since the time of the Founding Fathers.

"What do you think of DC?" Cleo asked.

"*De gustibus non estdisputandum*," (in matters of taste, it shouldn't be discussed) Bob replied. Cleo laughed. They fell into the leather chairs and listened to the sound of their bodies making impressions in the old material. Bob ordered two dark beers from the bartender, whose black bowtie and white shirt reminded Cleo of Bob's attire in old photos. They talked about Daniel Ortega and Central America. After a few drinks, they walked about Georgetown and somehow found a playground by a brick school. Cleo saw the swings, and they both laughed. A man selling ice cream cone appeared, as if in a picaresque play. Bob bought Cleo a cone from the man who also wore a bowtie. Then, she got on the old metal swings and she swung so high that she almost looped the swing over the top of the swing set. Cleo swung and laughed and Bob laughed, too, ice cream spilling over his hands. They went to a couple more brass and wood old bars in Georgetown and then went back to Cleo's tiny, steamy room. They lay on the mattress beside the washing machine, listening to the summer insects and feeling the rhythm of each other's compass.

On Independence Day, Cleo and Bob woke up refreshed. They could hear the mumbling of the Lindemore family upstairs. "People are still trying to keep their kids from talking to me," Bob sighed. Cleo washed up in the makeshift bathroom, changing into her tie-dye. They headed out the brown basement door, across the trimmed lawn to the red, white, and blue bus. There were numerous Deadheads on the buses to RFK Stadium, and the energy was electric. Patchouli oil and pot filled the democratic air of the Nation's capitol. All of a sudden, the bus stopped. The streets were clogged and buses could go no further. Cleo stared out the window. It was Bobby. Cleo wanted to go back, or stay on the bus, but the Black bus driver rushed the Deadheads out of the stifling capsule. They exited the bus. Bobby smiled as Cleo and Bob walked off. He had been following the bus, walking alongside.

"Bob, this is Bobby…Bobby, this is Bob," Cleo said, sheepishly.

"Robert Lee Purcell, of the Bazoo Purcells," said Bobby, extending his hand, Bob shook it.

"Robert Treat Paine, of Boston," Bob said, his hand stiff.

"Well, you have fun, I am going to hand out literature," Bobby said. Cleo quickly escorted Bob away.

"He's a little young for the Sons of the Confederacy," Bob said dryly. Cleo shrugged.

They walked up to the stadium. The day was sweaty, a typical swampy DC day. Cleo handed her tickets to the young ticket takers. Somehow, after they entered the gates of RFK, they ended up in the infield. Their ticket numbers seemed irrelevant on such a steamy day. Cleo twisted her blue bandana and wrung out the bottom of her tie-dye T-shirt. Bob took off his shirt. His hair and beard were full, a fuzz of almost childlike hair. Cleo asked a woman in a gypsy frock to take a picture of them. Cleo noticed that Bob's belly was taught over his leather belt. The concert commenced with no talk of this alarming sight, or of the meeting with Bobby.

"Garcia's 'noodling' on the guitar," Bob laughed.

"Shut up, hippie," Cleo laughed.

Bob Dylan sang '*Lay Lady Lay*', and Cleo and Bob held each other.

"Where have you been my darling young one?" Bob sang, his voice cracking. "Why doesn't he sing that one?"

"Not the time for it," Cleo said, leaning into their oneness. As the last strains of the 60s softly played to a stadium full of jocks, politicians, interns, and a few aging hippies, they exited the stadium. Cleo and Bob took the full DC buses back to the Northwest, stopping off for a drink or two. In the morning, Cleo dressed in the blazer and headed to work, dropping Bob off at the bus station. Mrs. Lindemore stared at the couple walking to the bus stop, mouthing something Cleo did not understand. Cleo paid her rent. She knew that.

9

The summer was almost over and Cleo bought a bus pass to travel the country. Bob had moved in to a communal house in Belchertown, living with some alternative culture people he worked with. Cleo took the bus up North to spend the weekend with him, hitchhiking back and forth into town. One night outside of Amherst, coming from a late folk concert at the Unitarian Church, they waited for a ride for an hour. Finally, a Ford van stopped. The van had a sliding door, a precursor to the current suburban minivan. As they scrambled in, they had to fight for a place with the baby seat in the back. The government had just started initiating the regulations on strapping in the babies. As the New England night air came through the van windows, they exchanged small talk with the driver, a pot-bellied father. Silence fell as if before an execution.

The man's voice changed to a deep place that went into the molten bowels of earth.

"How much for her?" the father said. The inside of the car went silent.

"She's not for sale," Bob said, suddenly becoming his father. "People like you are why we are losing the dream that our forefathers believed in," he added. "Let us out now." Cleo knew that people of Bob's age were all having families, and drove in safe cars. They stood by the side of the road in silence. An animal made a noise. A stream gurgled.

"It's OK," Cleo said. "We can walk."

As they walked in the Western Massachusetts night, Bob said, "Once, when I was 14, I was hitchhiking home from Boston, after a late night at a jazz club. The man who picked me up stopped under a dark underpass, and pulled out a gun. He asked me to suck his dick, 'or else.'"

"What did you do?" Cleo asked.

"Lumita, I burst out crying like a baby. I just sobbed, and then, he let me go." Cleo tried not to think of it. She was dancing her way through with blinders on. She finally felt like a bit of an insider, and she did not want to see what was inside of that world.

10

Cleo had to hitch-hike down to catch the bus for the rest of her trip. She stepped out of the Victorian house in Belchertown and put out her thumb. A small red car came screeching to a stop. “I have to go to the dump first,” the man with the scruffy beard said, as they pulled out. He drove at full speed to the Amherst Transfer Station. He pulled into the back of the property past old machinery and scores of blue plastic canisters. The scruffy man enquired, “Wanna get high? He pulled out the lines on a cigarette pack and Cleo put her nose down and the powder went up. It was the 80s. Coke was around like glasses of wine at parties. Cleo felt the rush. The man took a line and smiled at Cleo. “Ready to go?” the man chimed, reaching down to the shift. He, thankfully, pulled from behind the garbage dump and drove through the wonderful singing weather to the bus station in Amherst. Cleo got on the bus to see America.

Cleo passed the tobacco fields that she had once worked in and she was high. She was heading to all points south and west, sunny places, never to live in North Mills again. Cleo was once again in the gritty Port Authority, with a ticket to Miami in her hand, smelling pee and hearing the wails of junkies. She realized that this was no ‘see the US’ tour bus. The bus pulled through DC again, and she could feel the South emerge. Cleo tried to read some French poetry, but it did not sync with the smell of diapers and vomit. She looked out of the window and saw a Bojangles Chicken and Biscuits sign, with its cartoon-like pictures. A man slid into a car like Bo and Luke Duke’s General Lee in *The Dukes of Hazzard*. Cleo looked, but there were no signs on the drinking fountains. Cleo thought of her father on that bus in Carolina. He had told Cleo that he rode in the back. She too was riding in the back, but it was because it was closer to the bathroom. There were choices, options that were just not available to all two decades ago. There was not a Middlesex, Harvard, Hampshire, or Amherst student in sight, and, despite the cramped quarters, Cleo liked it.

The bus moved on into the South, past post offices, warehouses, fields, farms, and Winn Dixie Supermarkets. As the bus stopped to let people out in little and big towns, Cleo smelled fried foods. Nights were full of fitful sleep and odd dreams of slaves and the search for the Fountain of Youth. Finally, the bus pulled into the Miami outskirts. Bob's best friend Donald McDonald, or McD was likely somewhere in that state, his eyes glued to a spreadsheet at a hotel office, looking for losses and gains. He would be waiting for the three-day shift to end, so he could comfort his mother and see a few mobsters at the local dive. The families and the twitching addicts decamped the bus. Cleo saw distant boats bobbing in the sparkling water, perhaps boats that brought the very substance she had consumed before her trip. She stepped down into Florida. As she was looking around for the correct streets, a person spoke in Spanish to her. Cleo replied in French. The person smiled. Where Cleo grew up, you only spoke one language.

When she returned to the bus station, Cleo instructed the counter agent to write another long ticket, from Miami to Los Angeles. She enjoyed watching the agent write the names of many cities into the ticket. She went into the bathroom, picked out a bunch of paper towels, wet the towels with water and soap, and went into the stall. She then went to the sink and washed her hair with Herbal Essence shampoo. The bus pulled out of Miami heading for points West. Cleo woke up in the Panhandle of Florida. The dark night through the huge state was full of gas stations that read, 'Rebel Gas, 88 cents a gallon.' The stores sold rolling and chewing tobacco as well as bait and tackle. Old T-shirts and hats with funny sayings hung from the racks at the Stuckey Stops. The bus crossed over into Louisiana, and Cleo talked to a man who was heading to military training in Texas. He explained that there was nothing for him in his little Florida town, and he was going to 'see the World'. Cleo looked over and saw people reading *Playboy*, smoking and drinking beer in the back of the bus. From time to time, people came with boom boxes, playing music and partying. Cleo washed up when she could and watched the unfamiliar landscape go by. She saw kudzu vines and numerous billboards for truck stops, gas stations, and Gator farms. The accents changed, and Cleo heard the sound of French once again, but it was different than the sound she heard in DC. The towns were smaller and the bus rolled on. It was night when the people piled in at New Orleans, and the bus was completely full. Cleo smelled swamp and looked around to see the distant architecture of curled balconies and shutters. There was no music, but still there was a beautiful sound that came from the different voices. Cleo knew that she would be back.

The bus passed into Alabama and into Mississippi. It was dark and Cleo stared out at the oak trees. Cleo was feeling that the Janis Joplin she was listening to seemed to be missing something. Even Electric Flag wouldn't do. Then, there was Texas. Cleo really wanted to rest, but the bus kept going and going. She could only see vast grassland and then what appeared to be a desert. The small gas stations, train track crossings, and water towers with the names of little towns passed by. More soldiers got on the bus, along with many Mexicans. Then, the bus slowed down in the middle of the highway and pulled to the side of the road. A white vehicle with a green logo pulled up to the front of the bus. The wheels of the bus crunched in the dirt. A man in a green uniform came up the steps, an officer in uniform following behind him.

"You all citizens?" he asked. Cleo clinched up. She knew her mother was not a citizen, and people had spray painted 'Chink go home' in front of her house, but America was Cleo's home. She fumbled in her old army bag. Cleo had a bankcard and an expired Middlesex ID, but no passport. She almost peed in her pants. The officer walked down the aisle of the bus, his boots squishing like every one of the passenger's hearts. He asked if they were citizens, and they all replied in their best English "Yes." He looked at Cleo. She hadn't washed her hair in days. "What is your name?" he asked.

"Lu…Uh…Izzie Sugarman," she said, with what she thought was a New York accent.

"OK," the officer said, "we're not the SS." He laughed a cruel laugh. Cleo shuddered. She realized that a woman with a baby had gone in the bathroom, and she gulped for air, as the bored officer looked the bus over. Cleo made a mental note; tans were not sexy in certain circumstances. The bus pulled through the last of Texas and Cleo stared out the window at shacks on the Mexican side, taking it all in. She held her army pack close to her and ate her old bread and apple. The bus moved through New Mexico, and she saw her first native cacti. The plants looked sparse, with their spikes and dry green arms. The sun was brighter than any sun Cleo had ever seen.

"Hey, what tribe are you from?" Natives turned around in their seats.

"Um, the tribe of Tokyo," Cleo laughed. She did not even know where in that city her family lived.

"What the hell?" they laughed. We know you gotta be half of one tribe." Warmth spread over Cleo. She was different from other people and yet they accepted her for being different. She was 'in the tribe'. The bus crossed into remote scenery that went on and on. Cleo stopped in Tucson with its Spanish style churches and the sound of bells. The bus kept going through the long, long desert which was hot even at night. Cleo's mouth was parched. Cleo saw the sign for Interstate 15 to Nevada. She laughed and she could hear Bob saying, 'I knew the 60's was over when Grace Slick played Vegas.'

Finally, after four days, they pulled into Los Angeles. Cleo got out of the bus and walked out and onto the streets. Her 70s TV views of James Rockford, California Fever, and her visit last year to her RA's home in Westwood were not filmed or experienced in this section of the City of Angels. Cleo pushed the garbage out of her way with her boot. The stench mixed with the visuals of old sleeping bags; Woolworth bags in shopping carts and rotting teeth. A man sitting on the pavement passed her a paper bag and the bottle. The smells swirled around and Cleo thought that she could see the characters in Chinatown pulling levers to flood them all. That afternoon, the bus climbed out of LA like the snake on the Mexican flag. Cleo saw the colors of the city out of the back window. Time was suspended and the purple, smoggy air looked as beautiful as the accents sounded. But Cleo was not ready for the indigenous world yet. She got out in San Francisco, and she took the Cal Trans out to Menlo Park to see her friend JB from CALFORCE. JB was as white as one could get, but he wore a leather-fringed jacket and had a wide smile. He asked about Bob and hugged Cleo as if it were 1969. But it was 1986 and they were sitting in the living room of a Menlo Park ranch house with two new cars in its driveway. The Silicon Valley was about to emerge and stock trading would soon go crazy, but Cleo figured that John Cipollina would still be playing Golden Gate Park for a long time. Cleo and JB went into the City and danced and drank as friends. Unlike Bobby, Duane, and the man in the van, JB did not touch Cleo. When they returned in the morning, JB's mom, dressed in the same tennis wear as the previous night, was holding onto her bottle as the drunks had in skid row.

The bus left the city, going north towards less populated, more remote parts of the State. Cleo watched the scenery of the West unfold before her. The tiny mountains of New England seemed like hills. The bus turned east, and Cleo watched the flat, flat spaces with wheat and grain elevators go by. The people on the South Dakota bus were more sedate. The greasy smell from convenience store food stayed in the Greyhound and on the traveler's clothes. The smell stayed with Cleo for life.

The Greyhound began to enter the more populated Midwest. Chicago emerged, singing its own music of skyscrapers and shining water. The bus passed the parts of town that seemed stuck in time, with the corner stores, pizzerias, bars, social clubs and dance halls. Cleo thought of her anthropology professor, Cooper, and his work with the Chicago Vice Kings. She saw some graffiti that looked familiar from his book. She shook out her rubbery legs, got out of the bus and walked around the city. She listened to European accents, street language, and the sounds of a region whose tough weather made tough people. She walked through neon and trash, but also through the sidewalks full of business suits and briefcases. There was no time for tourism, so Cleo stopped for a beer and a slice of pizza. She talked to the overweight men next to her on the barstools, listening to their stories.

When Cleo arrived back in DC, Bobby took her to feed the addicts in Dupont Circle, but there were not as many people as usual. The whole city seemed on the verge of some bursting. On Monday, Cleo went to the educational association to say her goodbyes, finish some projects, and talk to everyone. She walked into the crazy Babylon of back room dealing, privilege, internationalism, and protest. "Let me show you something," Bobby said. "Let's get on the bus." Cleo and Bobby took the city bus to the business district. Cleo looked down to see a gaping hole in the city earth. "They burnt down the Capitalist Bank of America," Bobby said. Cleo knew that it was time to leave that city.

11

The leaves were turning, and Bob was moving back to Boston. 1986 was not what it was a decade ago, and Amherst had less opportunity. Life was movement; new places, buses, trains, and rides in cars. Cleo received calls from Bob in Ed Boykin's room, as she now had a single room in the dorm, but she did not have a telephone. One day, Bob called and said that he had spent the night at a construction site in Boston, ironic for a man whose family had helped to build the city. Cleo was measuring bones from long dead creatures in the physical anthropology lab. She was doing formulas, teaching kids how to apply to college, and helping them to stretch their bones, which were very much alive, further into the future.

Cleo was out late on Thursday night at the Witching Hour with Harold, a townie who was in the heavy metal band Panjia. He walked Cleo back to her dorm from the WEDU studio. They were laughing. Harold was wearing his black leather jacket with chains on the shoulders. They walked through the door into Cleo's hallway, a generic 1960s industrial construction. "What was that?" she asked Harry. "Sounds like smashing glass." Cleo thought of it as a hallucination of one of the heavy metal songs Harold had just played. The smashing got louder, and through the glass door to the outside, they could see some figures. Debbie came rushing out of her door, with her curly hair mussed from sleep. "I've called Security," she said, "It's been going on for a while." Her cute Disney nightgown was wrinkled. That summer, Debbie went to the Disney College Program and had her room was filled with the Disney motif, as well as the occasional Economist Magazine. 'How dare these people?' Cleo thought. She had been in the tobacco fields, the tough sections of San Francisco, the Haight, DC, where she had knocked a man down, and she had been around the country now. 'Who would mess with this hall? Who would scare Debbie?' She was ready to find out.

The Security Guard came strolling in. He was a small working class guy in a white uniform with a badge on his chest. He did not carry a gun, as that was verboten at Middlesex. He timidly grabbed the handle of the glass door to the outside of the dorm. He looked way less intimidating than Cleo's brother Hoke, or Hokusai, who had also been a night security guard. The three men stepped into the light. She saw her former part-time companion, Duane, flanked by his two fraternity brothers.

Harold looked at Cleo and asked, "So you want me to do something about this? I am ready." Harold had spent some time in jail, and he was known as a fighter in high school. This would not play well in Peoria, or with the Middlesex honor board or the Middleton cops. They had dealt with Harold before. Although Cleo had waited outside the Middleton Dunkin Donuts at 2 a.m. while Duane had been called a 'nigger', she knew who would get cuffed in this situation.

"It's OK, back off, Harold,"

"There's no problem here," Cleo said in her new Middlesex voice. "Harold Le Blanc is just going home to Professor LeBlanc's house."

"What are these glass shards?" the security guard asked.

"They slipped," the frat boys said.

"We were just walking by to the frat and they slipped out of our hands," one of the boys said, with a perfect prep school voice. Debbie pulled her robe over her Disney nightgown, and the security guard looked over.

"So everyone please be on their way," the guard said in a shaky voice.

Harold walked away, and the guys posed for a few minutes, then turned away. Duane looked clearly at Cleo. She was tired. Violence had been a part of her life in North Mills, and she was beginning to see that protests could not stop the groups in Afghanistan that her professor talked about, nor could they affect the people around her. She wanted to go to Boston to party.

12

"Duane was really good this summer with the kids. You know he's good with kids," Budkin piped out of nowhere. Cleo was tucking in her 'proper' button down shirt and Joe Astienef smirked. Cleo could not afford a car of her own, but grabbed the keys for the college van and headed out to Meriden. The van lurched and slid. Joe grabbed the wheel. Cleo calmed down and forced herself to figure out how to drive in winter. She had to take control, putting new rap music on the small radio and heading out on the icy streets.

Bob called her that night. He told Cleo that he was moving into a house, but to be careful because the guy who ran it was a 'ladies man.' He was paying his rent by playing the communal guitar on Friday nights. As the 'hippie/communal' culture waned in the late 1980s, less people wanted to share their cars for rides to Boston. Buddhism was not being taught at Middlesex anymore. That Friday, Cleo knew immediately what she would do. She got her army bag, collected her homework, and said goodbye to Ed, Mary, and Debbie. Cleo walked down the long hill and stepped onto the silver and blue commuter bus to Hartford. She then transferred to a bus that took her to East Hartford, a place where she had worked cleaning offices in high school. She walked by the side of the road to get to the I-91/I-84 interchange, the interchange that, in high school, represented all that she could not have. Her life had stopped at the Founders Plaza insurance buildings in East Hartford. Now, she hauled Bob's guitar, fresh from a California pawnshop, and pushed her army backpack further up on her shoulders. Cleo looked at the garbage and the intersecting highways above her. She stumbled a bit by the side of the highways, her foot almost grazed by a hypodermic needle. The cars and trucks whizzed by. That Friday, Cleo was optimistic, and somehow knew that she would always get a ride to Boston to see Bob. She fingered her bracelet with metal studs, 'to rake across people's faces'. Harold gave it to her two days before. Cleo wore it under her army jacket. She adjusted the bracelet as a Lincoln Town Car pulled over to pick her up.

"Don't you worry about men taking advantage of you?" the man in a black business suit said as Cleo sat down in the deep leather passenger seat.

"I'm not worried about being attacked, because I have this," Cleo said as she pulled up the sleeve of her army jacket. "I also carry a gun," she added. Harold and his sister had not just given Cleo a bracelet, but also a New York attitude. The scared businessman did not speak or look at Cleo, but sped up the highway with the News Talk station on his radio. When he dropped Cleo off in Cambridge, the announcer was discussing Reagan's cuts to welfare. Cleo ran down the steps into the T, taking it into Kendall Square, where the Greenworks office was. Cleo reached the office three hours early. The youthful college student secretary made Cleo wait on the used chairs. She sat, shifting in the uncomfortable seats, reading her homework, an article on the Buzkashi in Afghanistan. The office seemed warm and full of hope. Cleo's eyes were closing when she finally heard steps coming up the long set of stairs.

The first person Cleo saw coming up the stairs was Mark Bedan, a skinny man dressed in mismatched thrift store designer clothes. An Asian man wearing army fatigues followed him up the steps. He had a face that Cleo had only seen in movies like Kurosawa's *Dersu Uzala*. He was the mysterious and intense Rhys Ito. There was a contingent of Brazilians, including Luciano Reis or Luc and his girlfriend, the lovely Sunne. A man named Gerry LaPierre, a skateboarder of French Canadian extraction from New Bedford ran up the steps after Sunne. Fifteen-year-old Tim Olevskin followed him. Like the Brazilians, Olevskin's documents somehow mysteriously allowed him to work. 'Crazy Eddie' a Vietnam veteran, harrumphed his way up the steps behind them. Carolyn Elsing, an adult canvasser, entered the office, breathing heavily. Mark Williamson was the man who had invited Bob to stay at the communal house, Palming Street, in Arlington. He beamed as he came up the stairs, humming a song. He looked like a man from an outdoor leisure magazine ad. Bob had warned Cleo about the Welshman, who came from a privileged family and had sailed across the ocean with his father. Looking at his traditional good looks, and accent, Cleo was not attracted at all. Mark was seeing April Mulroney, who also followed into the small room. April was a student at BU, who had an attractive, rosy-cheeked appearance. Unlike Carolyn, she had always been able to afford a doctor. April's counter cultural wardrobe was always well appointed. The boss, who was collecting the night's proceeds, was Paul Hibban, a happy go lucky, relaxed office director, head of the odd crew.

Bob gave his money to Paul and cleared up his records. He looked over at Cleo and smiled. She was patiently waiting in the folding chairs. They walked out into the Boston night that had an oddly English fog wisping though the sidewalks and colonial streets. The old restaurants, landmarks and bars were still there, and the 'prodigal son' had returned. They got on the T, which moved its green cars through the underground, heaving and squeaking as if ready for the scrapyard. They popped out of the T, exiting into the Cambridge night. They were full of the moment, bonded by the music of subway musicians and encapsulated by time. "Can't believe that it's still here," Bob smiled. Jack's was packed that night. He took Cleo's hand and they went through the door. The bouncer smiled. Cleo later realized that he had waived the cover charge. Mark, Gerry, Rhys, and several others were at Jack's. The club was smoky and loud. Bob lit up a Marlboro and pulled some Bacardi from his jean jacket. He took a swig and offered one to Cleo. She felt all the Middlesex students smoothly slide away as she followed Bob to a table in the back of the club.

"I wonder if Jaco Pastorius is performing." Bob said. "I used to see him all the time in Boston." It was, in fact, Jaco's last year of playing. He would die at thirty-five, a genius stifled by a mad rush to find the Gods. Cleo and Bob would see Jaco soon, his drums flying like him, moving off into a haze of smoke. That night, however, Little Charlie and the *Nightcats* played. Bob and Cleo sat close to each other in the crowded recesses of Jack's, which, like Jaco, would later burn down in a frenzied gasp of the end of the 80's. Gerry fumbled over, grinning. Mark Williamson was the star of the show in the club, talking with everyone and enjoying his pint. The music was feel good blues, not like the heavy old sounds that Bob and Cleo had listened to in San Francisco.

"I don't care about the issues," Luc said. "Just give me the money." The whole crew laughed.

"So climate change and rainforest destruction mean nothing to a man from Brazil?" Mark asked. Luc shrugged and went off to dance. Cleo grabbed Bob's hand and pulled him up. He took a puff from his cigarette and got up on the dance floor.

They all went back to 18 Palming Street, the communal house in Arlington. It was one of those double decker houses on a side street off the bus line, only a few minutes from Harvard Square. Gerry and Mark were roommates there. Sarah Jacobs, one of the residents, was up and let them in to the house. Sarah was a red diaper baby. In her twenties, this woman was already graying.

"I see you have a guitar," she said. "Can you play Nanci Griffith?"

"Of course," Bob said. "But do you have the lyrics?"

"I do," Sarah replied and went to get them from her desk. Bob pulled out the guitar Cleo had retrieved from him from a San Francisco pawnshop and the sweet sounds of Nanci Griffith's music filled the room. People turned their heads. Bob played *A Hard Life*. A young man with curly hair looked up.

"Oh, that guy, he's from Maine. He's in the Witness Protection Program," Gerry whispered. My eyes moved about. Luc was climbing up the wall like an acrobat and a woman named Manik de Bourgeoisie was staring up at him. Manik, Gerry said, worked in the animal experimentation lab at one of the universities. A kid with 'Tufts Vet School' on his T-shirt came in the door and Cleo tensed, thinking that that might not be a good fit for conversation. But Gerry took out his thumb piano and began to play African music. Cleo thought about how Middlesex was not like this. These people were living on their own. Rhys looked over and Cleo realized that he too, was different than her fellow Middlesex students. Rhys, Mark told them, was not a citizen, so, despite his knowledge of ten languages, he had to attend Suffolk University and pay for the tuition on his own. Rhys did not speak, but he nodded his head and hummed to the music.

That night, after the party wound down, Cleo wore Bob's leather jacket to bed and made love to him on a cot outside of Mark Williamson's room. The light was low and Cleo looked over at Bob's face illuminated in the Cambridge moon from the window. Generations of features showed up on his face, like a past life reading. Cleo saw a confidence based on signatures by quill pen on parchment, teaching lessons but knowing that there was a preliterate teacher that pre-empted the Protestant sermon. His touch soothed Cleo like the feel of cobblestone and mortar.

A couple of blocks away from Harvard stood the Bow and Arrow Biker bar, where cocaine was readily available, and Harvard students drank on the front stools of the L shaped bar. In the back portion of the room, Bob and Cleo sat beside tattooed and bearded bikers. The bikers wore leather jackets with 'Lakeside Sharks, Laconia, NH' printed on the back. She looked at the jukebox, pool table and dartboard, which was right next to the bathroom. Bikers and their associates dodged the darts as they went into the narrow bathrooms to do cocaine. The Labatt's Blue sign, the Schlitz sign and dim hanging lights provided enough of a glow for Bob and Cleo to scope out the scene and talk quietly to each other. The bikers did not consider Bob a hippie or a WASP, because, since his early years in Harvard Square, he had developed a street scruffiness that was not simply the acting of a rich kid slumming. Ben Affleck and Matt Damon would later be sitting on those very stools in the movie *Good Will Hunting*. The bikers would be forced to merge into the Hell's Angels, like any difficult business merger that was cooked up next door at the JFK School of Government. The developers would put a weight loss center in the corner where the pub had once stood.

After an early winter afternoon at the Bow and Arrow, Bob took Cleo to Beacon Hill, where they laughed at the people walking by. Bob stopped in front of two white granite row houses overlooking the Boston Common.

"Why are we here?" Cleo asked.

"Oh, just paying a visit," Bob said. He leaned in towards Cleo, who wore a flowing Indian dress with ripped leggings. Bob wore a jean jacket and torn jeans. He whispered to Cleo.

"OK...OK...I'm ready," Cleo replied.

"UP THE ASS OF THE RULING CLASS!" they yelled in unison at the people coming in and out of the building. The people stared at them and moved quickly away.

"UP THE ASS OF THE RULING CLASS!" they repeated.

"Just like Curley," Bob said. Cleo looked over and noticed that Bob was wearing a white button down underneath the jean jacket. They began to laugh and laughed on and on and then kissed openly in front of the building's windows. Cleo later learned that this was the Somerset Club, located at 42–43 Beacon Street. The private social club was founded in 1826 or 1852, depending on your source. Bob's father had been a member, as had his grandfather and great grandfather. The club included Hornblowers, Crowninshields, Thornes and Coolidges. Members had left for the Union Club in the 1850s because the Somerset Club refused to speak out against slavery. At the time that Bob and Cleo were yelling at the two white buildings, women and minorities had yet to be admitted to the club.

They left the scene of the crime, holding hands and virtually skipping down the street; a restrained skipping, of course. They walked for a bit through the Boston afternoon and then took the T back to sit on the banks of the Charles River. Bob pulled out a big Elsie's Roast Beef from the pocket of his jean jacket, the greasy wax paper crackling. They shared the sandwich and a Miller and watched the Harvard crew teams go by. Bob then took Cleo to drink at Leo's Place and Charlie's Kitchen, 'old guy' bars that held the last of working class Cambridge.

Each weekend had surprises in store. Cleo waited for the group at the Au Bon Pain café, where she often danced with hippies in the rain. Women and men would play music and spin around the area in front of the café, just across from the entrance to Harvard. Cleo loved to watch her long skirts flow around to the sound of hippie music. She got soaked to the skin in the rain; her eyes dripping with water, spinning around in what Cleo thought would be an endless dance.

Some nights they left the hippie life and the warm confines of Palming Street, the Boston Food Co-op and Passim. They took the T and buses to Wally's in Roxbury, near Columbus Avenue. In the 1960s, Wally's was almost inaccessible to white people. Boston in the 1980's was still segregated in its own way, but students and jazz aficionados went to the club. The bus driver stared at the couple. Bob had not brushed his hair and, as he put the coins in the fare box, Cleo could smell the cheap beer and cigarettes on his breath. The driver sighed, knowing that any hatred for the oppressor could not include Bob and his dumbstruck companion. The bus pulled away through the late fall of 1986. It moved in an unending motion to where the Boston cops had drawn lines in the sidewalks and streets.

Cleo was now traveling on night buses on both sides of the country. She was going into neighborhoods that had been awash with blood on billy clubs and had, just years ago, been filled with the sounds of the spouting of epithets. The ride reminded Cleo of the ride on the buses to the tobacco fields she had worked in. But Cleo was no longer the supervisor of anyone. Silence loomed over the ripped seats that made Cleo feel like a useless liberal going to a university where epithets were banned, but hurt and difference was not a stranger. The couple sat on the damaged seats and did not speak, taking in the silence of night and the beauty of struggling people. Their faces were lighted orange like the nearby subway and the last of a day that was making reflections on its broken windows. Cleo looked out at the doors hanging off their hinges and the liquor stores and churches that hummed. "I have brought you out to see the blues," Bob said as they exited the bus. "But jazz is entirely different."

Bob and Cleo got off the bus. They walked and came to a door that also seemed orange in color. Cleo saw black iron bars on the small window. The couple entered the smoky interior of the club. She looked up at the framed black and white pictures of jazz musicians and the chalkboard with the drink menu. The musicians seemed packed in with them, nodding and touching people on the shoulder. They hefted their instruments on stage as if they had been hefting them since Prohibition. Cleo and Bob sat down and Cleo knew that this was the beginning of something. Perhaps it was like learning to read a classic literature and then proceeding later into reading its many genres and subgenres. The first straight up version always has an impression. Cleo looked over at Bob, who did not look tattered at all, but was classic himself.

Cleo did not see any students there that night. The lines were defined and the musicians played in complete synchrony. There was no question as they tapped their feet. Bob looked perfectly content as he ordered cognacs. He gestured, and a waiter came over. The night glowed smooth as if it were the 1920's. Cleo felt lifted out of her body, and then returned. She had been operated on, the ether oozing her into a dream state, and then returning her. Bob touched her hand. "There's a song. The song is called, *I love you more than you'll ever know,*" Bob said.

Cleo nodded.

"No," he said. "You don't get it. More than you will ever know."

At 2 a.m. the couple left the club. The men hanging around outside nodded at Bob. He asked a man for a Kool. He surveyed the scene and then gestured at a cab, which they could just afford. They got in and moved through the dark, watching people on the corners living their lives as those in the Somerset Club, but with more honesty and vigor. The got off near Palming Street and entered the house. The party was on, with its mix of the hubris of the East Coast college students and immigrants and young career canvassers with hopes for a better life. Cleo and Bob talked to people, but felt themselves lift to the top of the stairs and to the cot where they made love like the magic they felt at Wally's.

The Combat Zone was the area of Boston that was filled with strip clubs, mafia joints, and white ethnic bars. Bob had frequented the Combat Zone as a youth. The halo that surrounded him kept him safe. The area between Downtown Crossing and Chinatown had been a 'respectable' Red Light District up until the 1980's. There were clubs like the Pussycat Club and porn theaters and peep shows. Old men betted with the bookies and go-go dancers made their living. The owners knew the clientele and the microcosm was its own little family. In 1986, however, Bob was no longer a slumming student. The gentrification of the end of the century was yet to occur and no students risked themselves in the cold Boston night. In the 1980s, crack cocaine and gangs filled the one-block streets of the area. Bob brought Cleo back to a place that was quite different from the Combat Zone of his youth.

The couple quickly passed by a strip joint and a porno theater and entered the creaky red door. They made their way through the smoke to a seat at the billiard hall. A balding and chubby Puerto Rican cop got up from the end of the bar and sat beside them. His belly was falling over his belt and he was unshaven. His body made a sound as it hit the stool.

"How are you doing?" he asked, looking straight at the couple.

"We're fine," Bob replied in a steely voice.

"Well, I like to know all of the working girls around here," the cop said, staring at Cleo.

"This woman worked in tobacco fields so that she could get an education to not be ignorant," Bob said in a classic voice.

"Tobacco, that's hard work," the cop said. His face blanched and he looked away. It was as if the dictator's son was telling the soldiers to leave the compound. Bob stared down the cop as the couple finished their Millers. They went back to Palming Street, silent as they rode the T.

"My gutter life sometimes is not romantic," Bob finally said.

"But I love you," Cleo said. Cleo hardly thought of race or class, except for when she read about it at Middlesex, or when self-proclaimed 'gay' Sarah wrote love letters to Bob. She left notes to Bob on his cot that made fun of Cleo's working class connections and ended with phrases in French. This did not bother Cleo much. But after her time in the Combat Zone and other 'prime' sections of Boston, and with going back and forth to Middlesex, Cleo was beginning to think.

13

In the winter between 1986 and 1987, Cleo got an 'externship' at the Father O'Leary Refugee Program in San Francisco. Bob refused to go with her to the Bay Area. Cleo sighed and got on a People Express flight from Logan Airport. When she walked about the city, San Francisco seemed shinier, as if a big cleaning had been done since the summer months. She needed a couch to sleep on, but no one from CALFORCE was answering the phone.

Cleo walked from the Bart station to the Tenderloin, the area with the peep shows and strip joints. She saw a milder version of the Combat Zone. After the millennium, even the Tenderloin became gentrified. Then, the neon and piss was mingling in Cleo's senses, and the prostitutes walked around on high heels. Apparently, the big cleaning project had not reached this section of town. The transvestites pushed up their big chests and junkies huddled in the corners. Cleo had little money from her jobs. She went to one of the cheap hotels with a broken neon sign and made a payment of five dollars to the stringy clerk. Cleo went up the stained metal stairs and put her backpack down. She looked at the windowless room. She smelled excreta and saw a couple of cockroaches. She lay down in her new element.

The cafes in the town and Cody's books and the Berkeley Bowl were still full of tripsters and odd characters. During the day, Cleo was learning how PTSD could be used as a legal defense for refugees, but at night she was letting off her own stress. 1986 was turning to 1987 and Cleo refused to think that another decade would soon be at its end. Gerry Garcia and Merl Saunders were still playing at the Saloon. The Grateful Dead were playing the Oakland Coliseum.

14

When Cleo returned to Middlesex, makeshift shanties were set up on the green. Students from the dorm, whom Cleo had no interest in, would ask her to go 'hang out at the shanty.' Cleo refused to 'hook up' at the protest site. Making a move on someone while witnessing against a horrid, violent regime was not her speed. Like new fashions, there was always a cause for the rich students to protest. Cleo saw some of those same students in the career center picking up pamphlets from Morgan Stanley.

One day Cleo saw a flyer on her dorm room wall that read, 'Make Middlesex Divest from South Africa.' After staying up all night writing a paper on the Rough Rock Native Demonstration School, Cleo followed Middlesex students in a huge wave to the front of the Administration building. She yelled, like she did in DC. The crowd swelled and she sat down with many others, blocking the steps to the building.

"Go limp, go limp," a student with a curly mop of hair yelled. The students crunched down on the steps. The bored Middleton police held out their plastic cuffs. One fifty-year-old, graying officer pulled out his plastic cuffs and sighed. He half-heartedly grabbed Cleo's wrist and put the cuffs on her. Cleo went limp. The officer rolled his eyes, grabbed her shoulders and dragged Cleo into a van. The van drove the students down the hill to the Middlesex police department. Bored technicians and deputies processed them through. Somehow, she knew that she would not lose her financial aid. It was something about the softness of the cuffs; they felt bourgeoisie. The next week, she went before the honor board and told them that she had acted alone, and not as part of a group. She indeed had not gone to any of the organizational meetings with the spoiled students. The honor board's 'sentence' for Cleo was 'community service' hours. It seemed easy to fulfill. But Middlesex had its own apartheid, and Cleo did not have her passbook papers.

While she had trouble affording groceries, her psychology professor Davison was in his element as he chartered the protest buses to DC. One of her fellow students, a Latina had just joined the 'Young Communists'. She was Puerto Rican from the City, and Davison was beside himself with her authenticity. They were Communists riding in style. When she got off the chartered bus, Cleo saw Bobby and walked among the protestors, but the protests seemed somehow passé. Bobby's eyes were glazed over as if he was in a cult. As Cleo's 'Consciousness Development' class progressed, Davison would take the class to these protests or to meet with Soviet students at the Ukrainian Hall in the City. He always had things to do in the City, Cuba, the Soviet Union, and other Communist leaning places. Davison and the other students, Cleo knew, lived well.

15

Back in Boston, Rhys got exhausted at the parties and the partiers would carry him like a mascot up the stairs at Palming Street. But Rhys was getting closer to Bob spiritually and intellectually, speaking in snippets of the ten languages he knew. After April broke up with Mark, she also slept with Gerry. Then, Sarah saw her at the Boston gay pride parade. Sarah was marching with the bisexuals. People were creating new selves. Mark Williamson hooked up with Victoria Dotson, a woman from UMASS. She was majoring in anthropology like Cleo; but, unlike Cleo, did not need to finish her degree.

"Did you hear?" Gerry asked, coming out from his room at Palming Street. He was carrying his skateboard. His French Canadian features moved like the board.

"What?" Cleo asked, looking up from a cup of coffee.

"Victoria is pregnant. Mark has proposed and we are getting ready to go to a wedding in a few months." Cleo's stomach fell. San Francisco changing, Bobby Lee, everything was moving quite quickly.

The rest of the year went fast, but the mellow management of Greenworks was changing. A new apparatchik from DC named Harry Berson replaced the boss Paul, who was on his way to Berkeley to study Physics. Travis Brookman and Dave Preston, WASPs like Bob, got fired for stealing. Such acts were unheard of for Bob. It might be OK to steal from 'the Man', but one should never steal from a group that was 'working against the Man'. Harry Berson was a cocaine addict, but he clamped down on the drinkers and 'the fun'.

One morning, Cleo was having coffee in the kitchen, getting ready to take the T to hitch-hike back to Hartford and then take the commuter bus to Middleton.

"I've got herpes," a woman said. The woman was a new roommate at the house. She had an athletic figure, curly hair, and a Mediterranean face.

"I'm so sorry," Cleo said. "These men are lowlifes. You meet them at a concert and they don't tell you anything."

"He wasn't a low life as we see it," the woman said. "He has a PhD and is the head of a research facility." Cleo sighed. She left Palming Street with her books in her bag, realizing that all the people and movements that she was trying to academically label had little real world application.

Every weekend, Cleo hitch-hiked to Boston. She took the T's and buses everywhere and she felt like Royalty around Bob. They went to the Channel and the Rathskeller and the Plough and Stars. Despite the changing couples and the increasing office pressure, the office and the house were a collective group. There was always someone they knew who was playing in the band or working at the club.

16

Cleo heard the scream ring through Palming Street. It was the scream of an animal trapped in a corner. The wailing went on and on. She was getting ready again to leave out the door on her hitchhiking trip, eating a slice of luscious Gouda cheese that democratic socialist Sarah sometimes bought. She ran upstairs to Bob. They listened and quietly waited. Sarah came up the stairs.

"Gerry's sister killed herself," Sarah said. "I am calling into work and going home with him."

"We're so sorry, is there anything we can do?" Cleo asked. Bob looked unemotional, but Cleo could see him straining.

"Not now, just be there for him," Sarah said.

"We will be," Bob said. Sarah went down the stairs.

"I used to deal with suicide a lot in the Haight," he said. "There were so many."

"Why would somebody do that?" Cleo asked.

"You'll get it someday," he said. They held each other and went down to comfort Gerry, who had just gotten off the phone. Everyone gathered around him as family. The office, however, was changing, and many were deciding to work elsewhere in the summer. The suicide and its aftermath, the herpes and many other things began to make the spring seem hotter, and made the world seem more urban and densely populated. The next weekend, Cleo arrived as usual. "The people from New York are here," Gerry said. The high producers from the Manhattan Greenworks arrived and one of them was staying at Palming Street.

Bob began to hang out with the part time junkie Mike Nargo.

Mike had the word 'Revolution' tattooed on his knuckles and he talked a mile a minute. Mike said that he could kick smack if he went out to the great woods. The cities teemed with needles, mad music, and the end of a generation. The spring of 1987 was coming to a close and Boston was full of flowers in the parks and punk music and skaters in the streets. Mike's disheveled black locks and muscular body moved frenetically up the stairs at Palming Street. He carried a copy of *Ringolevio* by Emmett Grogan. He and Bob stayed up all night at Palming Street talking about politics, literature and how to kick drugs. Bob had kicked hard drugs a long time ago and was giving Mike advice. Every weekend, Cleo would come up the Massachusetts Turnpike, carrying her 'Science in Society' and 'Psychology of War and Peace' texts. She hefted Mandela, Gandhi and Aldo Leopold up the steps of Palming Street. That Friday, Sarah was at the kitchen table with Mike and Bob, smiling. Cleo joined in to the conversation on Reagan and the economy, but she wanted to go out with Bob alone. After a few weekends, with Bob playing folk music and people gathering around him for hours, Cleo began to worry about 'sharing Bob.' He was an intellectual and musical hot commodity.

"We'll go out together tonight," Bob said. They went to a Middle Eastern restaurant in Harvard Square.

"I like Mike and Sarah, but Mike is dependent," Cleo said, dipping her pita in hummus.

"I know," Bob said. "He's really intense and deep, but sometimes it's hard for me, too. But we are all leaving this office because things are getting too controlling. It's just for the summer, but a few of us need to get away. We need to go west."

"Wow," Cleo said, "Another town? That's a lot of moving."

"I know you like the West, too," Rob said, "It is less class stratified."

"Well, I guess you are right," Cleo said. "I love the Pacific and the mountains."

"I promise to spend time with you, too," Bob said. He began to sing, Floyd Dixon's *Hey Bartender,* Cleo raised her slice of pita.

The options were Boulder, Colorado and Eugene, Oregon, far from the quickly emerging nouveau riche of the cities of the East. Bob had heard that in Oregon, they hardly sold hard liquor except in state run stores. He was in. Cleo wrote a grant.

•

17

The anthropology department gave out grants for studying cultures. One woman was going to Las Vegas to study prostitutes, Jeni, the thin Thai/Italian, was studying the Grateful Dead tour, and others were studying Native Americans or inner city cultures. Cleo wrote a grant to study 'political groups and hippies on the West Coast'. They gave her $900. With the money Cleo would make from working, going door to door, combined with this grant, in a few weeks Cleo would make more than in three months of hard labor in the tobacco fields. Bob had already taken the train to Eugene. He and Mike had met up and were living with David Wilson, who had worked at the New York City office as well. David was a wild man from the hills of Massachusetts via the South. He had a brother named Gary, an illiterate Vietnam vet who had been poisoned with Agent Orange. Cleo purchased another Greyhound ticket and headed out.

18

Cleo was somewhere near Redding, walking on the street.

"Hey, you were on the bus?" a guy with a leather jacket and tattoos inquired.

"Yeah," Cleo said. They sat down on a bench. The large man started to talk. The man said that he had just gotten out of prison. Unlike many at Middlesex, his voice was gentle.

"Well, there was a shoot-out at the Motel, and a SWAT team," he said. "I had to do it," he said, "I took the fall." Cleo knew about taking the fall. He continued, "My Dad is actually in law enforcement. The first time I was arrested, he took me in the car and my Mom booked me; sad isn't it?"

"At least they had jobs," Cleo said.

"That's why I want to go straight," he said, "You know I am part Native American, and I had to decide in Prison, and I had to decide white."

"Me too," Cleo replied. Oddly, she had never discussed her race with Bob.

He continued talking, "I was in the Navy and I learned to weld, and that's what I am going to do now, weld things together."

"I am trying to change myself, trying not to 'sell out,'" Cleo said. He laughed, looking at her backpack and hippie gear.

"I travel all over the country, and I hitch-hike," Cleo said. "I have lived in San Francisco, DC, Boston, and I am going to Oregon now, oh, and I used to work in the fields…I just wanna be free. I love the open road, and parties…I've done coke, and I run a tutoring program…I go to see the Dead, Dylan, CSN, Van Morrison, Cipollina…and I totally pay for myself, no one takes care of me."

The man stared at Cleo, "Wow, you are a gypsy," he said. Actually, Cleo was hungry, because the grant check was being sent to Oregon.

"I am going to study hippies," she said.

"Are ya gonna sample the goods?" the man laughed as they saw the bus pull out. Cleo got up to chase it, but it was too late. "Ha, we are 'stuck in Lodi,' or somewhere near," the Big Man sang, laughing, "looks like we are stuck with each other…I guess I will be late to Portland, to see my family," he said. "I am getting out of it." He turned around. The patch on his jacket said 'Hells Angels'. Cleo wondered to herself and her mind quickly decided that he must have bought that jacket at the thrift store. An imitation, for sure.

"I gotta buy a new jacket," he said. What the hell, Cleo thought, she was stuck with this faker in a small town in California and why didn't she just "go with the lie." Maybe she could lie, too. He thought she was Indian.

"I am Pina Lumita," Cleo said, it was a name they had called her in the fields.

"I am Lone Jackal," he said, "Better known as Steven Atkins." Then, he took off his jacket to show Cleo the tattoo of the jackal. He had other tattoos, including a spider web on his elbow, which Coop had explained in class. She took a deep breath.

"Why don't you call yourself 'Deinotherium'?" Cleo asked.

"What?"

"If you went to college, you would know that it was a creature that was 15 feet tall and lived over a million years ago," Cleo said, "Now THEY were frightening."

"Almost as old as me," the Jackal said. "Or maybe as old as this first tattoo." He turned up his shirt and showed Cleo the tattoo on his back. He began to tell Cleo about the Angels.

"I am not into biker rallies because I am a hippie," Cleo said.

"A hippie that knocks a mugger down, takes coke, hitch-hikes, wears a leather band with spikes as a weapon, and walks the streets of dangerous cities in the middle of the night; I don't know," he said, "I'd say you are different, wild." They looked to the other side of the street and saw the sign for an 'All-You-Can-Eat' Buffet.

"I'd say that's all TWO can eat," he laughed. "They won't argue with a deinotherium," he laughed, but the Jackal took her arm and they crossed the street. He opened the door for her, pointing and waving his tattooed arm like a boy at prom. They ate greasy chicken and pizza and talked. People stared at them. As he spooned his peas into his plate, he asked, "You know that Skynyrd song, *You Got That Right*?" He sang:

'I see all the people wanna settle down,
You don't see their faces and they don't come around,
I'm not that way, I got to move along.'

"That reminds me of you." He smiled.

"Coming from an Angel, I guess that's a compliment," Cleo said. She had no house, no car, and no real address. Who could keep her down? Bob loved her, but they were having trouble finding a base. This man with his tattoos shared her outsider status. But being outside and having love is not enough, she knew.

That night, Jackal put his lumberjack style checked shirt on his big shoulder and let her sleep on that shoulder in the small bus station. This was no longer Los Angeles or San Francisco or Berkeley. There were logging trucks, lifted pickups, gun racks, as well as the occasional vacationing small van of eco-friendly people. Cleo did not feel that she was one of the eco-friendly types in that moment. She was angry with North Mills; mad at her teachers and at the people who had rejected her. The Middlesex students and their vacations and credit cards irked her. As the Jackal said, no one could catch Cleo. The Jackal was multiracial, too, and he knew the pain. No country clubs for this man.

Cleo spent a couple of days talking to this Angel. He told her over and over how, in prison, they forced him into a group. Cleo thought of Middlesex and the groups. The dining hall phenomenon – where in the dining hall, Blacks only ate with Blacks and whites, ate with whites. 'What would Duane think?' Her head was dizzy with thoughts of apartheid, the Communist professor who lived near the beach, Harold and his mixed family. The bus moved up California like a developing world train, puffing smoke and with bags tied on the bottom. Cleo's load was light then. Sonny Barger had not written books yet; he did not have a web site. People did bad things, but were still sensitive. These people talked to her more than the elite students who were too 'important.' Cleo wasn't interested in 'studying' this man. The bus went through the night and Cleo had her head on his shoulder in the front seat. He talked on and the sound was comforting.

In Southern Oregon, Cleo felt a change in environment. She felt a dampness that lasted for years. She saw cars pasted together with tape, sitting in front of old farmhouses that looked abandoned. In the late 1980s, this area was not a retirement and vacation mecca. Cleo knew backwoods. She grew up backwoods, but this was different. This was the end of America, close to the rugged coasts, where green leafy plants were the major crop and people guarded their crop with guns. Something sinister was afoot in trailers and broken down yards and swampy bogs. But something freeing was here, too. If you go far enough, the Ferraris don't follow, and the Tiffany stores know they won't make bank. The man next to her knew this. The two talked on and on, until, finally, they pulled into the Willamette Valley and

Eugene. Jackal gave Cleo his phone number and said, "You know if you get in trouble, I am there for you. My parents would love to meet you." Cleo knew that Bob's mom had called her a 'Jap' and that Bobby Lee's parents believed in segregation. Cleo smiled at the Jackal. They were both decompressing from a form of being contained. The light outside the cell was cloudy, but Cleo saw it, and the illuminated world involved movement and trees and was full of fish and boats and totem animals. They hugged goodbye.

19

Cleo took the public bus to David Wilson's apartment on a well traveled street in Eugene, a leafy town with a University, organic groceries, bookstores, and meth addicts. Cleo walked in and found Dave and Gary Wilson, with his red hair and USMC tattoo, waiting. Bob was out in the field working. The grant check had not come to the Greenworks office address. Bob returned in the evening. He hugged Cleo and looked into her eyes. He did not smell of alcohol. They settled into the old green couch, listening to traffic, early summer rain, and Gary's stories of Vietnam. They spent a few days hanging out, smoking the hallucinogenic Oregon pot. Cleo took notes for her study. But Cleo could not study as there were eight people crammed into the tiny apartment on West Eleventh Avenue.

Cleo came to Bob's office, which was in a building near the old grain silo and the highway entrance.

"This is the China chef," Bob said in a low voice. "That's what they call him, but I think that's racist." He walked in. He had a huge moustache, but he was not Asian at all. When the office went out together. John Gamble's eyes, when stoned, became slits.

"China Chef, drink another microbrew," the regional director laughed. John Gamble looked like an ethnic chef. Cleo said nothing, but John smiled at her over the table at McMenamins.

"Since you are cramped on Eleventh, why don't you guys stay with me?" John said.

The next day, Cleo and Bob moved into his apartment in Felony Flats in the Whitaker Neighborhood. John was no stranger to the needle, having been an MP in Vietnam, but he did not like 'junkie'

Mike, who had come out to Oregon before Bob.

"I am letting that junkie go," John said. Bob and Cleo met at the Tiny Tavern, across from John's apartment.

"But his numbers were high," Cleo said.

"Sometimes people don't like to be around people who remind them of who they were, my brother is like that with me. He took me to see Jim Morrison and the Beatles, and now he calls me a drug addict," Bob said.

Mike was soon working at the Genesis Juice Co-op. He was manic, and got into his job at the co-op as he had into making money for social causes. Bob and Mike often went out all night, talking philosophy and discussing *Ringolevio*. Cleo read through Mike's tattered copy of *The Basketball Diaries*. Mike had lived a similar life at the 'squat,' in New York City as had Mark Bedan. It was ground Zero in New York versus 'The Man'. On Cleo's way through New York, she had also seen the squat; the piles of rubble, political activists, and junkies soon to be replaced by boutiques and microbreweries and wine bars. No wonder, she thought, they were all in Oregon with its hippies, bored cops, and summer festivals.

Cleo got a job at Oregon Share, an organization working for the poor. She worked in Oregon's working class towns, discussing social justice. Working class Oregon was not working class New England. This was a tough turf. Although the people were pleasant, Cleo was somehow marginalized at Oregon Share. Ironically, being enrolled at Middlesex, no matter her class status, seemed to make the other employees nervous. John Gamble had previously run that Oregon Share Office. When Bob was out of the apartment, they talked. They sat on the ripped red mini sofa and watched *Magnum P.I.* They laughed over a bowl of pot, saying that they both knew what food stamps looked like. Cleo knew that it was as far from the Somerset

Club as anyone could get.

One beautiful June day, as Cleo was coming back from another slammed door evening of work, her eye began to hurt. She scratched it. It throbbed. She figured that she had just gotten some dust in it. Brownsville was dusty from field burning. She went back to the apartment in Felony Flats, and she lay down on the floor in a sleeping bag. Bob was out with the Wilsons. The eye began to burn and throb in ways that felt like torture. Cleo recalled how happy that she was when she first got contacts for her eighteenth birthday and thought of how the innovations had given her so much trouble over the years. When she did not have money to replace a contact, she would leave in only one, and try to read, go to class, and function with the sight in one eye. She knew that she was not going to be 'Marcie', as popular girls in high school called her, ever again. But this was different. Cleo began to cry softly. Bob and John came back, and Cleo told them, "I feel like my eye is on fire." They told her that she should go to the emergency room, but Cleo was so afraid of authority that she refused. She tried to sleep on the floor, but she could not sleep. The TV fuzzed out and her eyes throbbed looking at the Midnight screen. In the morning, Bob and John had to go to work. Bob told Mike Nargo to check on Cleo. At 11 a.m., Nargo came up the steps of Felony Flats, humming oddly. Cleo was whining softly, tears dribbling down her face.

"You need to go to the hospital," Mike said, "Your eye is full of pus."

"I can't, I can't," Cleo pleaded. "There is not enough money for the bill, and I don't know anything about health insurance. At Middlesex, I just go to the health center." Cleo had indeed gone to the clinic for maladies due to poor diet and stress. She screamed out in pain. Nargo ran out the door, running down the stairs, saying, "Stay put."

Nargo finally returned, grabbing Cleo's arms, lifting her off the floor. Cleo saw the tattoo on each of his fingers, below the knuckles, 'REVOLUTION.' With those 'revolutionary hands,' he pulled her down the steps. Years later, those hands would be cremated, like the revolution, in prison in upstate New York.

"Look, I liberated a car," he said. David's brown Chevy was idling below. "David does not know it," he giggled nervously. "I broke in, hot wired it, and here I am," he said. "I will call him later." Cleo stumbled down the stairs with Mike. As they pulled out, the Grateful Dead's song played. Mike sang it to her, *A Touch of Grey*:

'I will get By,
I will Survive.'

"See, Cleo, you will survive, don't worry." Mike hit the gas and sped downtown to the Sacred Heart Emergency Room, a hospital called 'Scarred Heart' by many. Mike burst into the waiting room, rushing by the security guard. He went right to the window, "She's dying," he said. "You need to treat her." The orderly, a tired Black man, put Cleo on a gurney, and rolled her down the hall into a cubicle with a white curtain pulled across it. A doctor with glasses, who looked about forty came in and stared at Cleo, with her mussed dark hair, and tie dye covering her tanned skin. He went over to Cleo and bent over, taking his light and shining it in her eyes. Cleo had chapped lips, due to walking so much in the sun.

"You've got herpes," he said, rolling his eyes, "You people and your lifestyles," he stated, and stomped out. Cleo knew that Bob did not even have a driver's license. Duane had potential, but he was not in her present or future. People at Wesleyan still had Palo Alto, Menlo Park, and Fairfax, Virginia. Cleo had an army backpack and now she had herpes. Cleo waited there alone for an hour and forty minutes.

"Hi, how are you?" a pudgy doctor came in. He was smiling.

"I have herpes," Cleo sobbed.

"Calm down. I am a specialist," the doctor said. He came close to Cleo, and said, "Whatever you have, you are going to be OK." He gently touched Cleo on the arm, left and came right back. He wheeled in his lights and some instruments. He came towards Cleo and the light pierced her cornea. When a light shined into Cleo, she felt so bared open, as if what she presented to the world was somehow false. She had no confidence that she was going to make it. Bob told her every day, "You are beautiful and talented and you will be successful." This was more than her family and people in North Mills ever told her. But Cleo had no help getting into law school, no money saved, and no idea where she was going to live when she graduated. She was laid bare, but she knew that she would have to see with one eye. The Mikes of the world, with all their faults, were going to have to be the ones who helped her, not 'the system'.

"Looks like a corneal ulcer, a scraping, "the pudgy doctor chuckled. "Damn amateurs don't know how to diagnose." He continued, "You are going to have to take drops and come every week for monitoring at Eugene Eye Center," he said. "It's a good thing your friend took you in, an hour or two more and you would have lost your eye," he said.

Cleo looked up and asked, "What about the money?"

"Forget about that, just take these drops and see me every week," the doctor said, leaning over and putting in the drops. He helped Cleo off the gurney. They walked out of the curtain together. The other doctor was hiding behind the nurses' station. By this time, Bob and Gary had arrived. The doctor looked and sighed, "No family here. I see."

20

John Gamble got let go from the Greenworks office. He told Bob and Cleo that the charges were 'trumped up'. Before he left for Seattle, he took the company car and pulled into Felony Flats. "Get in," he said. "I am the designated driver." John drove Bob and Cleo into the woods to Fall Creek, where they drank beer and sat in the water. Bob had fallen in love with the tall Oregon trees. The souls of the Natives, dead loggers, ranchers, trappers and scouts still drifted through Oregon. In a way, it was where Bob wanted to be – far from the cities and the ballooning banking/military/industrial complex. In Oregon, the people had shaggy hair like him, and the preferred drink was the new microbrew beer, not hard liquor. That Saturday afternoon, John seemed distant, watching Cleo and Bob. The couple were sitting on the banks of the mountain stream with their legs in the water, laughing. He approached them, sat down on the bank of the creek and sighed.

"They picked me and my siblings out of a lineup," he said.

"I guess we'll take him, too," the adoptive family said, pointing at John. Then, he discussed the adoptive family's discipline. They had taken a dog collar and a chain and chained him to the chairs for hours. Cleo looked at his 'China Chef' eyes. Cleo was never chained to a chair by a dog collar, but she had been chained in the same place for sixteen years. It had chafed her, too. She'd been called worse than a 'China Chef'.

After John left on the Greyhound, Bob and Cleo finally found a small rental house by the river. Summer was full of outdoor festivals. Every Saturday, there was a Saturday Market, which was held in downtown. People sold organic food, handmade items, and crafts. Tree, or David Richman, was there every Saturday selling his handmade joke books, spouting jokes with his green tree hat. He had bushy red hair, body odor, and a smile that revealed a few missing teeth. When the market shut down, Bob and Cleo asked the vendors for free food, and they always got vegetarian sandwiches, burritos, and Asian food. Many nights, they went to the Butte Tavern, and listened to Henry Vastine jam. Like his riffs, everything fell into their lap then, magically.

Cleo was not making a lot at Oregon Share, and the new Greenworks office was not working out. Everyone from back East quit. Bob and Cleo heard about the Peacemakers, a local organization. They went up the Peacemakers office, which was in the Growing Market Building, by the train station. Cleo saw a giant mural of vegetables and farms on the back of the building. The train rumbled through on the way to Los Angeles. Cleo and Bob went upstairs, where the offices of different progressive groups were housed. Earth First, a tree planting co-op, a lesbian newspaper, and several environmental organizations shared the space.

"Hi, I'm Dan Johnson." A man with gray hair and a gleam in the eye, greeted them. He walked them into the cluttered office. Gary Kitchens, from Woodstock, New York, and David Zuman were looking through a newsletter from the Nuclear News Bureau. A tall man named John Axline introduced himself as the head canvasser. Cleo and Bob sat down on the ancient green couch. "My Dad was Carol Doda's accountant. What accounts she must have had," John Axline said. It broke up the tension of a job interview. "There is no quota at Peacemakers," he said. "But we do sometimes ask for a pot contribution." Bob looked at all of the free progressive publications on the rack and smiled.

The following months, Cleo kept busy canvassing. John gave

Bob and her the good areas of town in the hills and by the university. Cleo interviewed the heads of the organizations for her anthropology project. In 1987, the office was full of tripsters, trust fund hippies, feminists, Eco-warriors and the like. This was the beginning of the new Eco-warrior movement, with people like Chant and Bobcat roaming the halls of the Growing Market. Ed Abbey's books were circulating, and Bob and Cleo read them. Like Abbey, Cleo drank beer and hung out with both the 'rednecks', like Gary Wilson, and the hippies. Cleo had become an insider.

21

"I've got some great acid," Dan Johnson said. It was a beautiful Oregon weekend, and Bob and Cleo were listening to jazz at home. The music filled the tiny rooms. They had just finished eating a healthy breakfast. Dan pulled in on his old bicycle. His shaggy grey hair and beard made him look like Santa Claus. He was bringing a bag of goodies. Bob had lectured Cleo before, "Whatever you do, do not do acid around me. I gave it up years ago. I reached a ledge with it."

"Dan and I are going to the university to party. Is that cool?" Cleo asked.

"Sure, the guys are coming over to watch the game," he said. In Eugene, Bob found that hippies also liked to watch sports. Even Tree had a favorite team. Dan and Cleo headed out on their bicycles. The rental house had even come with the use of a ten-speed. They stopped under an oak tree by the river. Dan handed Cleo a tab and she put it on her tongue. The sky was a perfect blue and the bike path was beautiful. They biked past the Rose Garden in Alton Baker Park. The roses looked as if they were from a magazine. Dan and Cleo began to laugh. They had been having many philosophical conversations on the back porch of Growing Market. They talked about the cosmos, politics, nature, the pollution of nuclear power and the evils of the military/industrial complex. Bob too thought him a 'new agey,' but was in no way threatened by him. After all, Dan was almost a senior citizen.

Dan Johnson had grown up in Oceanside/Carlsbad, California in the 50s. His dad was a drunken mechanic at Camp Pendleton who carried his bottle with him on the job. Dan's family lived in a mansion, which they called their little shack in the barrio. Their mother, Ruth Johnson, was one of eighteen children from South Dakota, so Dan's Dad was the option to get out of the cold. Dan learned to surf, to get addicted to speed, and to have his parents fund his physics studies at San Diego State. He was within one class of graduating when he dropped out. He ended up fixing planes in Thailand, drinking a fifth a day and sleeping with the Thai women. But as was typical of Dan's personality, he fell in love with these women. He was then able to call himself a 'Vietnam era' veteran. He, however, never bragged, and readily admitted his hatred of the war machine.

Dan and Cleo biked to the university. At the university, the sidewalks began to bend. "I never understood why people take acid in the city," Bob had told Cleo. "It's a drug for mind expansion and seeing the beauty in nature, that's where I did it, in the woods, on the beach." Cleo never had that kind of leisure time to go and just 'do drugs' for days on end.

Cleo and Dan walked by a restaurant, the Eagle Café, that had served her and Bob a rabbit stew at 2 a.m. the other night. No one served rabbit stew or acid in North Mills, Cleo knew that, which made her smile. She went to the bathroom. After she defecated, she got up. The toilet bowl was swirling, it looked like Munch's 'The Scream' and was now moving around liquidly. Cleo tried to wipe herself, but her hand was shaky. 'Where was her ass? Ah, there it was.' Cleo flushed and what she saw was a myriad of colors and shapes. 'Ah, human waste, what an amazing thing,' she thought, getting ready to walk out. She looked at her face in the mirror. The mirror moved as if liquid and her face moved, too. All of a sudden she felt claustrophobic, and the walls seemed to converge. Cleo had to get out. She ran outside. Dan was waiting for her outside, smiling. They walked to a dance club. Although it was afternoon, it was open, and its disco lights were pulsing. They walked in and the lights and sounds converged. Dan's white shirt looked electric. Cleo was so afraid that she would be like Fast Jack and the tripsters at the Pall Mall Bar in the Haight that she remembered. 'What if she never came back? What would my mother do if she did not finish Middlesex?'

Dan and Cleo danced on the floor, laughing and watching the lights. They then tumbled out of the club to see Tree, who smiled and told them a joke. He knew what was up. Cleo wasn't seeing God, though, or having revelations. She was just having a mind bend. Ken Kesey, who lived in this very town, had been a first experimenter with this drug at the lab at Stanford. Cleo knew that she could never have Nargo's Revolution on this stuff. The day was plenty full of light as they pushed their bikes around, heading back towards the river. They discussed nuclear issues, nature, and life. Dan began his profound talk, which people loved him for. This man knew about the universe, but forgot his kid's birthdays. The streets opened up. As they passed a fence, Dan took a branch and made a sound with it, going down the fence.

"It sounds like the helicopters in the Vietnam War," Dan said. "The big penis of war, striking."

"You never killed anyone, so you need not feel guilty." Cleo said.

"I fixed the war machines…I fixed the war machines," Dan stated harshly, pushing the stick against the fence. Cleo thought about Gary and his experiences and she held back what she was going to say. They passed streets like Washington, Jefferson, Polk, and, finally, they got closer to Adams Street and the house. They further passed by some fruit trees. The high was not frightening now, but beautiful. "Let's pick some pears," Cleo said. They grabbed pears off the tree as if they were manna. Cleo had bags strapped to her bike, and she filled them with pears. She filled her backpack with pears. She put pears in her pockets. They giggled as the pear tree looked like a religious symbol to them. The sky melted. They pushed her bike back to the house. Dan and Cleo then parted. He romped away with a grin and a few pears.

Cleo entered the house and proceeded to fill the refrigerator with pears. Bob was resting. Cleo was lying on the love seat grinning. He sleepily walked to the living room and went over to the refrigerator. The Frigidaire was filled with pears, top to bottom. Bob looked over at Cleo, "You are on acid, aren't you?"

"Guilty," she replied. Bob looked over like he could have been mad; but then smirked. He continued, "Pears? Whatever happened to acid and spirituality and revelation?" He went over to the stereo and put on Ornette Coleman. They went to bed and made love for a record five times, the music, the love and the high combining into a transcendental moment.

22

The Oregon Country Fair is an event that ought not to be confused with a county fair. It is a long running hippie gathering on the outskirts of Eugene that offers music, food, camping, theater, politics, and circus acts. Peacemakers had a table in the 'Community Village.' This was a perfect place for Cleo's anthropology study. Bob and Cleo did not have 'camping passes', but they were able to get in and see the action. Approaching the event, one could see the painted school buses and vans. Cleo saw a van with forty bicycles attached to it. She also saw a truck with a wooden cabin on its bed, complete with a stovepipe. John Axline pointed out 'The Merry Pranksters' bus. They went in to the fair and saw people dancing and laughing, playing mandolins and juggling. They set up a table in the Community Village, right by the Clearinghouse on Human Rights in Psychiatry and Hoedads, a tree planting operation. Ruby Begonia or Robert Larman, who was running his 'Get Fried Rice' booth. Willow came by to help and Tree was running around telling jokes. The eco-terrorists were yet to arrive in Eugene.

Bob snuck in some beer and had a cigarette. Smoking would later be banned from the Fair. All of the people in the group talked politics to people who were in agreement. The pot smoking made it seem like a three-day Dead show. But Cleo noticed signs like the ones she had seen in the Haight. Gourmet cafes wanted in. Cleo saw heroin needles on the ground. They heard rumors of costumed characters groping children. Cleo and Bob looked at the stilt puppets and the mimes and wondered. Bob turned to Cleo and said, "This isn't Seabrook," Cleo knew. She heard some of the men whisper 'abortion is murder'. As the drum circle drummed on, she heard some young men rating women and talking about sports. A 'hippie' took out his wallet with its credit cards. At the time, take away the one or two Black 'Rastas' and the few Natives, and the Fair would have the same racial composition as a White Citizen's Council meeting. Although Cleo danced to the music, and felt included, she still felt her alterity rise again.

The next big hippie event that summer was the 'Harmonic Convergence'. This was an event brought out to the public by Jose Arguelles and covered in Tony Shearer's book, *Lord of the Dawn* in 1971. This was the end of the 'hell cycles' in the Mayan Calendar that began with the conquest of Mexico. The gathering was held in a field outside of town. People from the office and the local community were milling about, hugging and smiling. Cleo looked at Dan and others and asked, "How come there are no Mayan Indians or Blacks here?" The group looked at Cleo as if she were a criminal.

Cleo shut up. A tall man began a chant and instructed them all to hold hands. "Let's try to end the hell cycles," he said. The crowd started to hum 'Om' in a circle. Cleo felt nothing. After the group broke hands, Cleo heard someone in a poncho say, "It's all going to change now, Bush will be out." Someone else said, "Yeah man, the Indians are in charge now."

Cleo went home and saw Bob with an empty six-pack next to him on the couch. He looked at her expression.

"Now you are getting it," he said. That afternoon, Cleo went to the Peacemakers Office.

"You have a message," John Axline said, "from Jackal." The 'Angel' had called the Peacemakers office, and Cleo knew that it was time to go back East. A few days before, she had seen on the news that the Angels had a huge gathering outside of Portland. Jackal had promised her that he would stay out of it, but Cleo knew that he was there. She realized that the people who 'lived outside the norm' had their own Social Register and gatherings. They could be easily found without a phone directory. There were the Grateful Dead concerts, political rallies, and gatherings. People could find her, too, and it was disquieting. Cleo knew that there were drug circles as well, and not just pot. In a lot of Dead Shows, 'Jose,' (not a Mexican, but part of their scene) was selling dangerous nitrous from unlicensed tanks with a fake business. The acid was bad and ecstasy and coke were the 80s drugs 'doing the rounds'. Meth was all over and having inroads in hippie Oregon. Cleo knew the places where these drugs were. At the normally sedate Portland Blues Festival, Cleo noticed Hells Angels jackets. It was time to leave.

23

The return to Middleton in the fall of 1987 came with its usual shock. At Middlesex, Cleo faced students who were meeting at the Career Planning Center, prepping for their Wall Street careers. She went to get LSAT information and saw students asking for interview tips and pointers. The previous spring, Cleo bid for a spot in on campus housing for a room. She was rejected from the Community Service House, so she got a room in a Victorian at 250 Cobb Street, a side street leading up to the campus. The Queen Anne house was at the corner of Pearl and Cobb and was built on the former site of the Middleton Court House. The house had three big gables and a wraparound porch. J. Peters Peterson had owned the property in 1883–1884. Her room was a tiny corner room, right next to a second stairway that used to be the servants' entrance.

That autumn, Cleo would wake up from the radio show 'The Witching Hour' with the heavy metal band 'Panjia' with puffy eyes, feeling sore and with the sun piercing through the shades of the Victorian. Stumbling downstairs, she noticed the maid, Emma, the black women who would wipe up the debris left by her roommates, exchanges from Mt. Holyoke, Wellesley, Smith, and Dartmouth. Emma picked up the gin bottles left by Peter Mills Miles Fivecoats and E. Tacy Trambridge, who could be heard bustling in the background. Bob had stayed in Oregon for a while to make some money.

"Cleopatra, are you coming to the Olympia Diner with us?" Peter asked, his head peering into the living room. Peter was not an Ivy League exchange student, but a model whose mother lived on Central Park West and whose father lived in Palm Beach. When depressed,

Peter and Cleo would play childish games and eat candy with her old roommate Mary. Middlesex did bring together different classes of people with different races and cultures. The three of them would hang out together in the Victorian. Mary cast them in her movie for film class. Peter played 'the waiter from Hell' (complete with an old waiter's jacket) and Cleo played an incarnation of the 'Spirit of Spring' in a white flowing dress. They acted well together, but, of course, there were differences. That morning, in front of Emma, her face got red. Cleo could not afford the Olympia Diner and she did not understand why she now stood out from the rest of the diners, people she normally would have fit in with. Peter, however, loved to 'experience it'. Moving towards the door, she nodded at Emma.

"Emma, you coming to my party?" Cleo asked, between bites of a three-day-old baloney sandwich.

"No, I can't do that, gotta work." Emma laughed, watching Peter leave. Cleo then sat as Emma rested in the living room. Emma had been warned against fraternizing with students. "This job aint so bad," Emma continued. "I remember tying up tobacco plants. I used to work in the fields of Carolina…it was hot under those nets… and tobacco juice be sticking under your fingers. I knew about the technique of tying up plants. Man, I still think it's there sometimes, the juice," she said.

"I worked in the fields, too. You know, it seems that I can't…wash it off," Cleo said.

"Look pretty clean to me," Emma laughed. Cleo sighed, remembering the pines the night that she had been out with a young man firing sheds. She could feel the willows grazing the riverbanks in Carolina, and she could see Emma, sitting under their soft, slow flowing.

"Look, Emma, take some time off, come to my birthday party…"

Cleo suggested.

"It wouldn't be right." Emma responded.

"I'll leave a beer for you," Cleo said. They both laughed and Emma headed out the door. Cleo saw the cars traveling by, up and down the street on their way to cocktail parties and fall tailgate picnics under the New England ivy. Cleo was going to Graduate Liberal Studies to work and then to the kitchen of the dining hall. She had decided to take a second job (the one she had promised herself she would not take when she entered Middlesex after years of grinding work). The future was uncertain, and, even if she got into law school, she did not know where the rent money was going to come from. Other students would comment on her overwork (the full class load and two jobs).

"Why are you doing that?" they asked.

"For rent money when I graduate," Cleo replied. They looked dumbfounded. Peter talked about the 'Round the World' tickets being sold for 'only $1500'. That afternoon, Cleo had answered calls and done Xeroxing at GLSP, and then she was taking the slop off of students' plates and emptying them in a garbage pail and putting dishes in the huge dishwasher. The good thing about that job was the free food and the fact that Cleo would put study materials on a ridge above the dishwasher, reading as she was putting the dirty plates in. After her jobs, Cleo went up the stairs to her room in the Victorian, on the second floor in what used to be the servant's quarters. She could hear her roommates. They were busy in planning strategies for landing the future executives from Greenwich. This was not her old dorm, with its lesbian anarcho-feminists and democratic socialists.

"Dave is from New Canaan," Margaret 'Peggy' De Ment, a Women's Studies Major, said over her tea. "He is going to be an advertising executive…that's why he is studying psychology." Dave was indeed in Professor Davison's class, likely because he thought it an easy A.

He nodded his head in class, but scoffed behind the professor's back after he left class, laughing at the ideas of social justice, protest, and the plight of the downtrodden. Cleo could see how one could laugh at the professor's 'Connecticut Coast Communism', but she still thought apartheid was a horrible law. Peggy had snagged her mate sunbathing in a bikini top on the porch of the Victorian. In their 'Men's Studies' class, Peggy talked about the myth of the vaginal orgasm, and the students viewed porn magazines to discuss 'objectification'.

Cleo showered quickly, dressed, brushed past her roommates, and took off for WEDU. As guest deejay for the heavy metal show, she escaped Peggy and the other's strategic maneuvering. The first time she had co-hosted with Panjia's and Harold's presence on Friday night, Cleo ordered pizza. Harold was paying. When the pizza arrived, she noticed that Harold was picking off the pepperoni.

"Why are you doing this?" Cleo protested.

"We are a vegetarian heavy metal band," Harold smiled. Cleo laughed at the incongruity, drinking some Schlitz Malt Liquor, letting it slide softly down her throat. "We paid a dollar for the extra item," Harold said, tugging at the sleeves of Cleo's thrift store jacket. Cleo did not even like heavy metal that much, but it was people like Harold who drew her to the scene – hard drugs, black leather jackets, and the removal of pepperoni. She knew that life quite well, that violent and intense song, with its natural element. When she was in North Mills, carrying a knife was not just for work. She had kept it under her pillow, carried it with a familiarity, a familiarity that families of junkies and pushers understand. Carrying this instrument, this pain, it was a strange fraternity that seemed to be understood by Harold's family. That night, Harold, Evan, and Cleo were drinking and eating in the little control booth of the radio station. It was 2 a.m. then, and she was wasted, gone. She managed to get into the blues section of the record library and was including some old standards along with Metallica. Luckily, Harold and Evan were too drunk to notice. She remembered the old prize fighters in bars listening to 'Champion Jack Dupree'. She played, especially for Evan and Harold, a favorite version of 'Wine, Wine, Wine'.

"Hey, let's dedicate one to the Communist professor," Evan slurred. "Consciousness Development." Cleo and Evan were both TA's for the class. "Not a bad guy for an atheist," Evan continued. And so they dedicated a tune to him. Cleo thought that she was hallucinating when she stared at the stacks. She noticed a figure in a suit jacket. How odd, she thought, for the metal show. It was her history professor, Professor James, who she had not seen in a year and a half. She had moved on to 'cooler' classes. Cleo noticed him and peeked out from behind some 'Metal Church' records. Cleo left the booth to go see him.

"Selfhood, ha…what are you doing here?" She slurred.

"I am getting some…jazz records," he said.

"Your tastes are like from the twenties," Cleo said. Even Cleo had taken on a little of the new, hated, *Valley Girl* slang. She continued, "Hey, I read that Reinhold Bendix about Max Weber…I mean it's… exciting," she said, pronouncing Weber as 'Veber', as she had heard Bob do.

"You'll get to like it more and soon…" the Professor laughed. Cleo covered her ears.

"Are you drunk?" Cleo asked.

"Lumita, I'm stoned," he said, slowly, using the first name Cleo never used. She laughed, as students and professors used to laugh at her.

"A Delphian gets stoned," she mocked.

"The blues aint bad," said the Professor, embarrassed and affecting a working class tone.

"You were listening?"

"It's all right, but don't dedicate anything to that Communist, promise?" Cleo promised him.

"Come see me on Thursday," the Professor continued softly, grasping his John Coltrane record. Cleo remembered the name Coltrane from somewhere. The cry came from the other room.

"CLEOPATRA!"

"SHIT, Harold...oops...is calling," Cleo hurriedly said. She whisked herself out of the record library to watch her buddy spin the tunes. The 80s was a time of easy highs and was breaking into a world of fast, tough metal, techno music, and MTV Madonna dance music. But the radio station had records of all music in its stacks, from the old jazz to the current new music. It wasn't that Cleo did not care for the Professor, Peter, and Tacy, but it was just that she was more comfortable with Harold and his sister Niema, who seemed to live a life without rules. Niema was different than Harold, who appeared more 'white', and played 'white music'. Niema, she looked black; she listened to what might be considered 'black music' and talked about her home turf, the streets of New York City. The first time Cleo had met, not run into, Niema, she was visiting Harry, and Niema was tripping on acid, saying, "You've got to come party with me...tell me about selfhood." Bob was still in Oregon, and it was unclear when he would be back to help her fight the battle with the privileged students.

"I will show you some spots in this place," Niema said. And Niema did begin exposing Cleo to the seamier side of the college town. As Cleo, Harold, and Niema got to hang out more and more, as an odd threesome, they became like family – the heavy metal musician and his leopard skin leotard sister. Cleo did not listen to warnings or advice much then. One of the Professor's daughters had seen Niema get in a lot of fights in high school, and there had been trouble with the law. Mary also cautioned that Niema was mean to others at times, speaking her mind directly and sometimes in cruel ways.

Cleo began to spend more time with Niema than with Harry. It was Niema's soft style of teetering on high heels and swearing at the world that struck her. She was the woman with the silent, strong father who filled the hallways. On weekend nights, Niema would guide Cleo to all the places she had discovered in her ten years in Middleton. They went to rooms in the tunnels beneath the college that could be found only through special access windows. Niema, Cleo, and Niema's boyfriend Johnny would bring 'jungle juice' and crawl into those little rooms. They would laugh and feel safe from any outside intrusion. They sought out small rooms that had only one way in. They also went to bars, small-time discos run by the Mafia, where they would laugh and hit the dance floor. Cleo expressed herself in ways she could not have imagined, even in Anne Greenbaum's Creative Writing class, which Cleo had somehow, at Mary's suggestion, gotten into. The public safety of the college never stopped Niema and Cleo, however, because they knew the man, the father. But Cleo would always return to the cut glass windows and the cornices of her other life.

24

At night in the Victorian, yearning for Bob, Cleo remembered her father showing her a clipping from the newspaper and talking about how he had tried to be a boxer, but he had been punched through the ropes too many times. And so, Cleo was determined, playing just like Peggy in her own quest for success, albeit a different type of success. She purchased a book to study for the LSAT. Other students were driving to the Kaplan course, but Cleo neither had a car to drive, nor the extra money to pay for the course.

Cleo recalled summers before Middlesex, slipping out of Andrew Valerian's blue Audi car as one slips into the ring to fight carefully. She thought that he would be the kind of man to offer her a way out. But, stumbling up the steps at her house, giddy from cheap champagne, she saw eyes, white pupils dilated and bloodshot, piercing out at her. She tried not to recall these moments, but when Bob was gone, her thoughts went back to Hoke, her brother, who stood in his greasy uniform. Hokes' eyes had settled on the shiny pearls that stood out from Cleo's fragile throat. Every night that she came back, she was being watched with silence, every move followed by the red and white eyes. As she was on her way to the library, she felt for the string around her neck that she used to wear in high school. She unexpectedly ran into the Professor. "Where were you this week?" he asked. "Roja, verde, amarilla," Cleo thought, "which one?" as she fingered the empty space on her neck. Her names from the fields came back.

"I was at…Harold's," she said.

"Harold's? I thought he was in jail. My daughter went to school with him and she said…" the Professor began.

"Your kids did not go to public school," Cleo scoffed. She knew that Professor Cooper's daughter had gone to Middleton schools, but not this professor's kids.

"Both of my children went to public school. They did, you know." Cleo raised her eyebrows and he admitted, "Only for a year." He then said, "Heavy metal, that's not even music."

"What?" Cleo replied sharply. "I get my work done, you know I got that grant for my research; what are you bothering me about?"

"Yes, studying a biker bar and hippies is not considered legitimate research in some circles."

"Reciprocity, life crisis rites; OK, we were thirsty," Cleo said. He continued to press her, "You've got to start drinking better wine. Is that why you have not been around?" he said.

"You finished that bottle of Maddog 20/20 I gave you for your birthday?" Cleo asked.

"I did, did you finish your assignments?" he asked.

"I did and they gave me the same kind of headache," Cleo said.

"The drummer," the Professor sighed. "I don't understand why he is so hard to approach. He wears those African clothes, and he doesn't speak to anyone."

"Harold?"

"No…I can't believe that you go over there. How is he? I mean, what's it like? Nobody goes over there except to take lessons," he said. Cleo did not understand why this man was asking her these kinds of questions – about some broken down house on the other side of the hill.

"What kind of lessons?" she asked.

"Drumming, jazz drumming," the Professor hesitated, looking around, "the faculty has been talking, he is not well." She understood now.

"He's like that guy O'Malley," the Professor continued, "he was not on the retirement plan, he just taught a few classes." Cleo had elevated her Buddhism professor O'Malley to a pedestal, having seen his books, but this other Professor was right, he was a Harvard mailroom worker. But Ed Le Blamc, jazz instructor, she would soon learn, was different. She remembered the reaction when the Neville Brothers had played on the college lawn and Harold and Cleo had been partying and dancing. Ed came by in his dashiki and Moroccan cap. Harold's father had talked to the Neville Brothers like family and Cleo said, "I guess the college administration is not that amenable to African clothing." The Professor then nodded, lowering his voice, "You know he played with John Coltrane?" Cleo was not sure who John Coltrane was. Then, she remembered the record held in the Professor's hand, but also a picture on the wall at Harold's house, on a wrinkled poster.

"I hear that he is going to play with Sagittarius Jackson again," the Professor said, "It's been many years."

"Sagittarius, what an odd name," Cleo said.

"So what is it like over there?" he asked.

"It's interesting," Cleo said, "a lot more interesting than when the class went to your house for dinner."

"Anything is more interesting than my house, Lumita," he sighed. But Cleo had no answers for the Professor. The LeBlancs were no ordinary family, she knew that. But she could not help saying, "See you later, DOCTOR."

"Don't mock me. I have tenure," he replied. "Why don't you come to the Asia House for some tea with me?" Cleo now knew that her middle name was printed on the rosters, and, despite her pushing her heritage away, people knew.

"No, I have research to do. Harold is my specimen…I will be

around the academic buildings more now, though." Cleo missed Bob at that moment; She needed some explanations and translations.

"Take care of yourself, please," the Professor said. "People miss you."

25

At the library, Cleo studied Levi Strauss, Hegel, and Weber. She spent hours indexing terms, cross referencing information for her 9 a.m. class. There were times that she would be up until 6 in the morning with the boys from the band, struggling to her morning class. The combination of drugs, lack of sleep, and tension would give her fevers, and her body would take long to adjust after every bought. She lay down in the Victorian after the library, where she was still ducking Duane, who would stop by from visiting his frat brothers. She would do four hours of homework, some partying, and would then go to Harold's house, where his father's eyes pierced into her. 'Those eyes, why those eyes?' She wondered.

In the kitchen, Tacy and Peter Fivecoats were having a conversation about the arts and humanities. It wasn't that she didn't like Tacy and Peter. Peter had even invited her to Manhattan and Palm Beach for Christmas break. But, like her relation with the Professor, she felt distanced from them. She was unskilled in their arena, her laughter regulated carefully and judiciously. Tacy's father had showed up once, in a suit and tie. He was from somewhere called Orinda. This was not the Tenderloin, or Oceanview, and Cleo knew that. This man was only ten years older than Bob, though. Peter did not care who was in the house, a man from Orinda or a kid from North Mills. He liked to sit around in a white robe drinking vodka. He had friends who placed a full-length mirror down between two chairs. They put a full line of cocaine down on that mirror and snorted it.

"I can see myself," Cleo said.

"I can see myself, too," Peter said. Cleo lit a candle and Peter teared up. "My mother...and her parties," he said, "Why...Why?... They live for those parties...and you know she has a $20,000 party and the next day she tells me I have to eat pasta, Cleopatra."

"Next time, clean 'em out, stash the food in your bedroom, under your bed...she'll never notice...she'll never notice, you'll eat for days... That's where I used to hide my food."

"But Cleo, the maids...then there was the time I watched my contact lenses go down the conveyer belt in baggage on the way back from Paris...she made me look for it...it's not like she couldn't afford another pair...Oh, and that horrendous Austrian boarding school, even made me miss Choate...Choate Rosemary Hall." Cleo kept listening. "Elizabeth came in my room from the window, she pushed herself on me, and she was heavy...I felt horrible...no one has sympathy for a man who gets attacked sexually." Cleo remembered that Peter had mentioned the issue of violence against men in 'Men's Studies'. People were scoffing. Cleo went down and made three of his blueberry waffles and brought them up to him and they discussed when Peter might go to the GBQ meeting – 'Gay, Bisexual, and Questioning' club. She could see why some of his friends did coke.

26

When Cleo watched Harold play drums, she felt the stellar rush that coke gives. It was cold in the graffitied basement of the house, where the band would practice and she would hold her bottle of Jack Daniel's next to her on the couch. She would not drink the whole thing; some of it was for show. They played songs from their new demo tape *Inception*. Cleo watched Harold in his black half T-shirt, quickly moving about the cymbals. She looked at herself in her ragged jeans and army jacket; wondering what his hands were like. She knew that she could not live without those sessions, those hours; moments away from the Victorian. But it was odd, since her meetings with professors were on Thursdays. It took her a while to adjust. Over the hill was a long walk, especially on a cold day, and her thoughts, her desires became jumbled. It was a good thing that Dave's Liquor Store stood between the two spots. Some days, the Professor would be nervous, almost shaking, other times complacent, together, and strong. In the office that Thursday, they had been discussing systems of reciprocity.

"You know it's like when you give to me, and I give to you…you know, I mean, when we exchange things," the Professor stumbled.

"Well, I am not sure I want to cover reciprocity." Cleo said. But he pressed, asking that she "think about it more." Cleo stared up at the books, at his face, all of sudden, with its Delphian profile. She flashed on high school, the image of the brain diagram cut in half. She recalled the way students threw spitballs and how they stuck to the teacher's pull-down visual aid. Cleo had laughed at the teacher for his pocket protectors, but he had nominated her for the National Science Merit Award anyway. He had been there to describe the symptoms of cocaine and alcohol withdrawal to Cleo on the phone, when people she knew were in trouble. Then, Cleo flashed on the pull-down diagram of the frog's reproductive system; it seemed to juxtapose itself on the very intricate map of the Political Systems of Highland Burma that she studied over and over for class. But she never let the Professor touch her; only touch her on the arm. She was waiting for Bob. The Professor would briefly hug her and then let go. In a sense, this was not the real world, either. There was a level of respect at Middlesex that Cleo never had before. Like maps on desks, the professors were required to be damn rigid about certain things. The Professor's body was straight and strong and accurate. Cleo would shake uncontrollably after his attempts at intimacy and hugging.

Cleo trembled on her way across the hill to visit Harold and Niema. Visiting the musician's house, however, she would not mind being touched. She heard the soft tapping in the background. Cleo never really listened at first. It disturbed her, the different types of sounds; the difference between the hard, heavy metal and the other rhythm, the rhythm of father. Like anything else when Bob was away, Cleo chose not to deal, not to let it in. But she could not help but be mesmerized by the sound…the heavy, the soft, like different breathing, like the essence of life. It seemed that the man was everywhere. Cleo leafed through the *New York Times* that was in the Victorian, and she saw him mentioned in an article. She saw pamphlets on the table of the college administration building with his name on them. She tried to block out the presence of his eyes, too, the figure; but it kept coming back.

27

As the autumn leaves began to turn slowly, like liquor aging perfectly, ready to be drunk, Bob called the payphone that was downstairs in the Victorian. He said that he had some news he needed to tell her in person. He was not going to return to Greenworks Boston, as the office had changed. He could stay at Palming Street only for a few days, so he was going to come down to Middleton. Cleo wondered what it was he was going to tell her. She was excited that they would live together again, but this crazy house with its many people was not like living in the Eugene house. Cleo knew that Jeni Comini, whose dad was a rich New Jersey businessman, and her man from Manhattan got rooms in houses with only a few people. The couple was allowed to have huge dogs. It seemed unfair. They lived in relative calm, Jeni reportedly receiving large shipments from New Mexico at the Middlesex post office.

In the early fall of 1987, Cleo felt a frenetic energy at the Victorian. She walked in the door after class. A resident of the house was twisting his locks of hair over and over and repeating something. He bolted up the stairs. It was Jeffrey Junkerman, who had taken up residence in the attic. Cleo went up the stairs. Mary was walking behind him. Jeff kept a futon on the floor. His saxophone sat beside it along with packages of pasta. Mary and Cleo looked to the corners of the attic where they saw trunks full of items. Mary looked over at Cleo. Cleo looked back. The dust moved about in the shadows and the autumn light. They pulled the latch on a trunk and looked in. Crackly paper and clothes revealed themselves. Mary reached in and took out a letter.

"My Dearest..." the letter started. The script was from the 1800s.

They heard a rustling in the other corner. All three of them looked over. Shivers ran through Cleo. Mary, like Bob, was able to communicate without talking or picking up a telephone. Mary ran down the stairs, screaming. As the year progressed, they would hear sounds in the room, even when Jeff was not there. This strange presence became a part of life at the house, but not as odd and seemingly made up as the other, current residents of the house. Henry Rawinger came into the kitchen. He was incredibly skinny and had a shock of unruly blonde hair.

"I got something to show you," Henry said. Cleo looked up. The Oscar statuette was gleaming. 'It must be a fake,' Cleo thought.

"My grandfather designed in Hollywood," Henry said.

"Let me see that," Peter said. He held it and looked it over.

"Wow," Cleo said. "But we gotta get to class." That day, in Men's Studies, they were again viewing pornography and discussing the objectification of men.

"Look at the size of that," Peter said to a shy, small man. The class went on to discuss male battering of gay males, and son's relationships with fathers.

"My father told me, one day you won't look that way, just you wait," Peter said.

"That's horrible," Cleo said, musing on the troubles of the rich and beautiful.

After her Psychology of War and Peace class, for which Cleo was a TA, she walked upstairs in the house and saw the young man from class leaving Peter's room. Cleo put her books down and went to the kitchen. Henry cooked endless bubbling pots of chili with odd spices. Cleo opened the lid of the pot and looked in to see the crazy concoction. Peter was in the kitchen with his friend from class. "We like to play with toys together," Peter said. "He has a lot of games and kid's toys. It's a turn on."

Peggy and her 'straight' boyfriend walked in. They were carrying some Wild Irish Rose. They could afford better wine, but had seen Evan with it and likely thought it trendy. It was all Cleo could afford. This woman's studies major's trophy boyfriend carried an umbrella and wore a raincoat in rainy weather. The alternative culture oddballs looked at him with disdain. They knew his secret, though. He was a transfer from Michigan State, not at all like those who had studied three years at Middlesex.

"That guy tries too hard to become successful," Peter said. "Part of my family is old money and I find these types to be..."

"I totally get it," Cleo said. "My boyfriend had all the benefits, but he never wanted to show it."

"I want to meet Bob," Peter said. They looked over and saw Henry and Jeff headed up the stairs to the attic. Their eyes were wild and their hair askew. "I've gotta go," Peter added. "It's time to party."

Emma the maid cleaned up the condoms, white residue, blood, spilled liquor, boiled over chili, and hateful graffiti that Niema had written inside the utensil drawer, mocking the privileged kids. Fellini himself could not have written the movie of just one afternoon in that house.

28

That year, Niema, Harold and Cleo shared a need to go far beyond the edges of their halfness as they could. They shared the smell of the street, the odor that could not be found on the other side of the hill.

One day, Niema and Cleo decided to go to New York City. It was Niema's birthday, and Cleo decided to spring for the cheap tickets. They picked up a bottle of Monarch gin, shivering as they drank it by the small bus station on Washington Street. The fire overtook their stomachs in the back seat of the Greyhound on their way through Connecticut. A huge box played rap in the background, Public Enemy's brash sound thumped. '*We got to fight the powers that be... we got to fight...*' They sang and laughed unabashedly as they played with the little children who moved between their arms and the arms of their mothers. As the city skyline knifed pinkish-purple across the river, they laughed and held onto each other, linked strangely in the third seat, which is tacked on next to the bathroom of Greyhound motor coaches. The Port Authority Bus Terminal was full of the usual nodded out eccentrics and pushers. That day, however, it had that desperate sense of warmth, like that warmth felt in those little waiting rooms where the homeless hide.

Niema was laughing, "We're home...we're here..." She stood up on the waiting room seat. "DO THE RIGHT THING!" she yelled. Cleo was dumbfounded. A chunky policeman immediately rounded the corner.

"You got crack, don't ya?" he yelled and jacked Niema up against the wall.

"Nope, just gin," Niema grinned wide. He poured the remains of the gin in the garbage, disappointed.

"He cheated me…I wanted that too…" Niema commented. They headed for one of the bathrooms, where they copped some cheap coke. They placed it out on a toilet tank in a stall and the feeling quickly filled that empty space in their heads. They finally extricated themselves from the station, walking drunk and drugged through the garbage, listening to men holler at Niema's beautifully shaped spotted thighs that tottered on those high heels.

"Kiss my half-black ass," Niema yelled, "Fuck them all." They tottered to the subway. Walking through the garbage and yelling statements at the world, was that what Cleo had paid for with those tickets? she shivered, thinking of the Professor and Political Leadership among the Swat Pathans, a complex social system in the Northwest frontier of Pakistan where centralized power was a recent phenomenon.

"Is this it?" Cleo asked Niema. The little letters stood out from the tunnel as they descended. They got on the graffitied subway that Niema knew so well, even while drunk.

"The museums are closed, OK? Relax," she said. They held onto the railing as the mechanism jerked its way through the city. The subway stopped and they fell out onto a platform and then out onto the street. "No Red Dog Saloon tonight, sister." Niema laughed. She was referring to the biker bar that Cleo had studied for anthropology class. The coke sharpened her vision. Cleo watched as Niema was strutting into the City. Disoriented, Cleo asked her where they were. "Where are we? We are in the Village. Not like African village. Greenwich Village, you know…" Cleo laughed.

"Daddy's playing down the street tonight, but we can't let him know that we are here." Niema continued. But Cleo knew that he knew. Niema and Harold always seemed to do that, mention their father at odd moments. It was as if the world was glued together with this man's life, but the specifics were never mentioned. It was just Daddy and his music. They walked into a corner club, with a wooden bar and a dressed up evening clientele. Cleo felt strange without her leather jacket. She missed Harold then, the way he was never out of control; the way he managed those drums, with force and precision. He had a slow way of speaking, too, that never seemed to alter. His vision was perfect. Cleo thought of how, on one of his most drunken nights, he had called her up to go to the station, and she wondered what he was up to. That night, Evan and Harold were sitting together by the mike, putting some records on. Cleo had watched the dials pulse.

"They can hear us all the way to Massachusetts tonight, maybe even New York," Harold said. Cleo wondered if he was fabricating. "Yeah, and it's a good thing we put some extra power on, because we have something special happening tonight," Harold lowered his voice. They stopped the record. He continued, "Tonight, we have our very special guest deejay…Evan, will you introduce her?" Harold spoke into the mike. Evan introduced Cleo to the audience.

"And we have something special for Lumita Cleopatra tonight." He continued. She gasped as they cut to a segment of Steel Prophecy, a new band Harry was part of. It was a solo of Harold's.

"Here you go," Harold smiled. She looked over and he handed it to her, "Suitable for framing." He grinned. It was a black and white pen and ink picture of a dragon and its eggs in a den, stalactites hanging from the ceiling. The picture had a womblike appearance, even with its sharp lines. On the picture, he had written, 'This picture is called Mom, Hope You Dig It. Anyway, Good Luck Always in Whatever You Do, Keep in Touch. Love, Harold'.

"Say something on the air," they had insisted.

Cleo stumbled and said, "Thank you, thank you guys, you are so kind..."

"We love you, Lumita," they told all of Connecticut. Cleo's mind returned to New York City.

"Aren't we going to have trouble getting home?" Cleo asked Niema.

"Don't worry. I know a few people here," she assured her. Cleo thought of Niema's image in the small college town and smiled. She watched her leopard skin sister stride to the band. "Let me sing, let me sing," Niema continued. The bandleader, in a crisp white shirt and bolo tie, looked over at her.

"We can't do that..."

"C'mon, I CAN sing..." Niema walked up to the bandleader, teetering. Cleo laughed, tripping over herself. But Niema got up to the microphone and sang. Cleo looked up at her beautifully formed fruited lips opening. The music was blurred, but strong and painful. Between the stage and the tables, Cleo danced gingerly and intensely. Verde Cleopatra, she remembered the wine and her name from the fields, Verde Cleopatra. At 5 a.m., the bar closed and they had nowhere to go, so Niema took the crowd with her – nothing better for a tigress than a 6 a.m. walk through Washington Square Park. They walked into a building with a series of small, closet apartments with huge locks on the doors and tiny televisions placed in the corners on cinder blocks. Cleo urinated in the bathroom just big enough for the rickety toilet – almost locking herself in. Cleo tried the lock again and again...she almost panicked, but managed to slide the catch back and burst out. She flushed and the whole building shook. They then followed a musician named Leon down the steps below the City into a basement apartment with no windows. Sitting on a pullout cot, Cleo listened to Niema and Leon making love. In that tiny space, Cleo held herself, hearing a singer revealing herself and moving to the sounds of the City. There was another person in the room, a small white person. Cleo could not tell if they were male or female. The person was lying against the wall, nodding off.

"What do you do in this city?" Cleo asked.

The person sputtered, "Leon…Leon let me stay here sometimes…I mean I used to…sing sometimes. What do you do?"

"Oh, well, I'm kind of a…traffic light," Cleo said. Shaking from the partying, she stayed up and reassured this frail, white person as they listened to the sliding of the trombone through the wall in Niema's city. During her senior year and even before, cocaine was free and ubiquitous on the scene. Cleo did not know all of the politics of this; the ugly story of how the cities were saturated by coke that came from flights from Central America. It was always around, and always free, not just for birthdays or trips to the City. It was an answer for a lot of things, riding from the pressure of life. One did not see pleasant visions on the bad stuff, the marginal coke. It was still a damn good high; the kind that jerked you into a state of not escape, but sharpness, intense sharpness that seemed to carry with it a command over the banalities.

Though one could see the ugly essences, one could feel the back of one's head splitting with an unjoyous, yet simply intricate vision of the patterns that one could seemingly manipulate. For this, one merely had to roll up a bill. Cleo had to study, and it helped, but she did not have the leisure that the other students had to relax and party all the time. But seeing junkies in the City with a pipe to the lips or getting the cream to cover their injection spots, was another story. It was grotesque and it repulsed Cleo. She understood the pounding need. It had been in her brother's red and white eyes. Niema and Cleo went to the crack and smack dealer's houses, the dark rooms where seedy looking men were playing stereos as large as the walls. One dealer had affection for Niema. He was tall and stout and dressed in white. He looked like a former football star.

"Hey, I got that Billy Holiday tape you wanted…aww, you don't even know Billy Holiday, anyway; Can we have a couple of lines to go?" Niema asked.

"This aint fucking McDonalds," he said, his huge form stretched out in the dim lighting. Cleo noticed a picture of Niema on his bookcase, her beautiful hair flying away from her eyes. Finally, he relented, and they took a share and went home.

29

It was a good thing that Bob was on his way. He was taking the train back East from Oregon. Cleo was tired. The pots clanked in the large dishwashing machine as she threw them in. She studied her note cards that she put on the ledge above. Her hands were raw and she was thinking about her next job at Graduate Liberal Studies. She looked at the clock. Bob was due that evening from Boston.

He had only two bags and his guitar with him when she met him at the bus station and walked with him up to Cobb Street. His beard was a bit longer. He wore flare leg jeans, a button down, and scuffed cowboy boots. They stayed close to each other and smiled. They walked into the Victorian and through the foyer towards the stairs. The exchanges from Wellesey and Smith stared at the couple.

"Hi," Cleo said. "My boyfriend is here." Peter came down.

"Hi, I have heard so much about you," he said. "You went to St. Paul's and Cambridge School. I went to Choate. Those kids are crazy," Peter said.

"Yes they are," Bob said. "But I am sure you liked some of the cute guys there." Peter smiled at Bob. They went up the stairs and into the room, where she let Bob lie on the futon. There was a knock on the door. It was Jeff.

"Henry and I are going to go for a drive," Jeff said.

"One rule of thumb," Bob said. "No driving while you are tripping, please." Jeff smirked.

"I guess you are right, we will wait until we come down." He left and went back to the attic.

"Sorry, I am kind of protective," Bob said.

"Like a hippie den father," Cleo laughed.

"Or maybe a tripster dorm parent," he laughed.

"Just wait till you see what goes on here," Cleo said.

"I've seen it before," he said, laughing.

Bob easily summarized the Soviet invasion of Afghanistan or the Palestinian/Israeli conflict so that Cleo could have conversation with others about the topics. She had plenty of food at her job, and Bob seemed to keep himself fed. One late morning in October, though, she looked out the window and saw Bob coming up the hill to the house.

"I was hanging out with the people on Washington Street," he said. It was the tough part of Middleton.

"What are you doing there, Niema said that she saw you," Cleo asked.

"You know, taking a break from the kiddies," he said. Cleo sighed. Bob responded to Cleo's queries later. "I did not want to ask you for food so I went to the soup kitchen." Cleo worried that the kids might dislike Bob for this.

"Tell me again about Winter Carnival in Quebec," Peter asked. "I always wanted to go there."

"It's European, but it has a funky, alternative flair," Bob said.

"What do you think Nabokov meant by that line?" Jeff asked, pointing at his paperback. He was learning Russian, but this version was in English.

"It's metafiction, there are stories within stories," Bob said. "There is so much Pale Fire in this house, creative and intense energy, but it's pale," he said. "Suicide," Bob said. "That's all I am going to say."

"Who do you think is going to make it to the playoffs?" a young Jewish kid quickly interrupted.

"Let's watch the game," Bob said. "We'll see how Ricky Sanders is doing." They went into the living room and turned on the TV. Niema walked in the door and over to Bob. She walked up to him and hugged him and smiled, her lip gloss accenting her huge smile.

"Saw you on Washington Street with the bums," she laughed. "You really know how to hang in the hood." He gave a slight grin, giving in to the hug. The Sunday went on with a sense of a placid picnic. No such family existed in the real world, with Jews, WASPS, Blacks, gays, straights and in between, walking with a ghost between the living room and the kitchen of the J. Peters Peterson house.

That afternoon, Henry sheepishly asked for condoms for an afternoon with a girlfriend. But Bob wasn't just there to hand out birth control. The students were dealing with bad tensions fueled by drugs, pressure about the future, and the 1980s push for success. When Bob was there, it felt more like the 1960s Middlesex.

30

"There's something I need to tell you," Bob told Cleo one Saturday morning, as they woke up smiling at each other. Cleo was tired from working and studying, and she rolled off the futon, rolling over a copy of Vargas Llosa that Bob had been reading. He helped Cleo to go to sleep the night before by reading Garcia Marques' *A Very Old Man with Enormous Wings*. Yes, life was magically real, and was about to get more magically real.

"Do you know who I am?" Bob suddenly asked.

"Of course I do, you are Robert Treat Paine," Cleo laughed. They had lots of jokes about WASPS and all, and it was fun. He asked her again.

"Who am I really?"

"A hippie, whom I fell in love with, and am still in love with," she said.

"You aren't listening," he said.

"Sure I am," Cleo said. "I know you pretty good; you saw Hendrix, you protested the Vietnam War, you went to Paris, and you had girlfriends with sexy names," she laughed.

"I am not getting anywhere with this, "Bob said. They made some coffee, and Bob put some liqueur in it.

"My father was born in the 1800s, Class of 1917 at Harvard," he said. "He was an officer in the Navy in World War One."

"I know that," Cleo countered. "And he was an asshole, who made you mix his drinks at age eight; he thought it was funny."

"There's more than that. He was in the Somerset Club, second in command at the Eastern Yacht Club, not the Corinthian or the Boston

Yacht Club," he said, his tone changing a bit, as if he were older, talking in a library with a lot of books.

"Yeah, you told me, so you broke out and you became a hippie, and that's whom I love," she said. "Let's listen to some Jefferson Airplane."

"I've heard it too many times," Bob said. "We used to have a bell that would call the maids. I can still hear it," he slowly continued. "We had stables, and a gardener, and stone lions that are the entrance to Paine Avenue."

"Oh," Cleo said, "You did not tell me that…I have to study for the LSATS and I need to write a paper, so can we get drunk later and talk." He was making her nervous.

"I used to listen to the Red Sox with the gardener," Bob said. "We listened to the transistor while he was working. My Dad would not take me, so he had the gardener drive me to the game at Fenway Park. He must have paid him to sit beside me…my grandfather had a Rolls Royce Silver Shadow, he kept it with the other cars, but they were all sold," Bob said.

"Oh," she said.

"My father had a license plate, so the police would not bother him; a plate reserved for only a few. My mother used to have vacation in the White Mountains, and the Prince used to flirt with her at the chalet… She saw Hitler from the balcony in Austria when she was studying there." He sounded sick.

Cleo just wanted to be with him and party later.

"She also gave Papa Doc her tourist dollar in Haiti," Bob said. He told Cleo about Duvalier, but he never told her that his mother had been there at that time.

"My father was a Brahmin," Bob said. Cleo often heard the word in reference to India, but now this was getting weird. "Boston Brahmins do not really exist anymore, but my father was one, and we were raised to be that way." She thought for a minute. Bob was polite. He read menus in French. But defining his way of being was like defining hers; it was not easy. Cleo thought of him as a hippie, poor and anti-materialistic. She thought of him in the little apartment in Oceanview, San Francisco, with friends like Southerner McD and working with bartenders like Kathmandu at the Pall Mall.

"My family has a curse," Bob said, "that's why I don't have kids…I need to tell you something," Bob repeated, "come over here." Cleo came to him and he took her to him, his arms around her. He smelled of Marlboros and the sea. "I know that you are worried about paying rent when you leave Middlesex, and you are worried about your student loans and how you will get around," he said.

"Yes, I am," she said, "But it's hard to think until I get through the LSAT."

"Lumita…somebody died," Bob said. The room was silent.

"I'm sorry, I hope it's not McD," Cleo said.

"They left me some money," he said, in an embarrassed voice.

"How much?" Cleo asked.

He whispered, "It was enough." It was not a million dollars, but it was more than her father made in her entire high school, and likely middle school, life.

"So, what will you spend it on?" Cleo asked, thinking that perhaps he would give to charity.

"I want to spend it on you," he smiled.

31

It took a while for the money to come in, and, to the chagrin of Fred Sargent of Gardner, Preston, and Moss, close to her 21st birthday in 1987, Bob requested the money deposited in the Farmers and Mechanics Bank in Middleton. Bob loved the way 'Farmers and Mechanics' rolled off his tongue. But the money did not come in time for the LSAT. On a Fall Saturday, Cleo was up at 4 a.m. and took three buses and a taxi to the test, which was held at a public high school in an obscure town. Cleo spent weeks trying to figure out how to get to the school, calculating the bus and taxi fare. She thought of herself riding her bicycle at 5 a.m. to the SATS in Simsbury, fifteen miles from her house in North Mills.

On a similar chilly morning, Jeff, Peter, and Henry saw Cleo off to the LSATS, confused that she was taking a bus. The day that she went off to the LSATS, Bob seemed sad, however, Cleo pressed on. She got out of the white Bell taxi, handing the driver a ten, which was so much money to Cleo. At 7:30 in the morning, she walked into the industrial type school building. She saw BMWs, Mercedes, Audis and VW buses parked in the lot. She also saw long-haired Middlesex kids get out of a VW.

After having paid an exorbitant fee to take the test, Cleo knew that she had to enter the green doors. Monitors were sitting at tables, packets in hand. Cleo took her packet and went into the assigned room. As the clock turned to 8 a.m., she began to sweat. She chewed her pencil. The numbers and letters swam in front of her. Cleo guessed, chewed on her nails, and realized that she never really had understood questions on logic. She knew now, the political systems of Highland Burma, Hempel, Garcia Marquez, the Psychology of War and Peace, and rebel Buddhism, but 'Each of the following could be TRUE except for X' made her think of the feelings of the person writing the question in a dark room. She wondered how much they paid the writer.

"Black Monday," Bob said. "They lost 20 grand." Cleo had no idea what he was talking about. The money was delayed as the brokers figured out the mess. Mark Bedan, living with his parents in Newton Centre, lent Bob $500, with interest. After a week of taking Cleo to breakfast, lunch and dinner, Bob moved up to Northampton. He went to the Bay State SRO for a while, occasionally staying at the UMASS hotel, getting students and alumni to rent him the semi-luxury rooms. On the weekends, Cleo loved staying at the university hotel, looking down on Amherst from clean sheets and the new cable TV.

"Is this Ali?" Bob said into the hotel room phone. Cleo heard a surprised voice on the other end.

"Remember me, Santa Claus, who drank the Millers, what is your address? I owe you for my tab and I will put some interest on the check," Bob said. Bob was settling his past and living in the now. Cleo tried to do the same. Several weeks later, she was shaking when she opened the envelope. She had failed the LSATS.

32

With Bob gone during the week, Cleo got paranoid in the Victorian, crippled with her fevers. The students would come closer and closer, like the Professor, only with their tennis matches and gin and tonics, or 'g and t's' as they called them.

"Cleopatra, come to Palm Beach." Peter kept insisting.

"Yeah, they will think I am the cook, you'll love it," Cleo said. Peter scrunched up his face and asked why Cleo was always gone on weekends.

When she was at Middlesex, Mary cast Peter and her in another movie. This intricate film, which Mary had written, costumed, and directed, was set in Victorian days and involved the filching of various outfits from the college costume shop. It was hardly filching, as Mary was likely the most talented costumer at Middlesex. Mary filmed and photographed Peter and Cleo, fully clothed in the empty bathtub of her 1920s house that stood between two cemeteries. Mary dubbed the house 'Blue Heaven'. Peter loved bathtubs with claws.

"I'm in ads," Peter laughed loudly, "I'm in underwear ads," he said. Cleo was trying to keep him from disturbing the people in the rest of the house, who were sleeping. He had done the same for her when she was agitated. She asked him which ads he was in. "I'm not telling," he taunted in a childlike voice. Cleo swore, however, that she had seen a similar body in those scandalous Calvin Klein ads that were everywhere. "Its good money," he said, "Your friend Niema ought to try…they are looking for that HALF look."

Cleo called Niema on the phone and heard her mom in the background, talking about Daddy. When she got to Fountain Avenue, she looked into the mom's eyes, holding her bottle hard. There were times when the paranoia got heavy, like a drug that got intense and wore off. Cleo would come back to the Victorian shaking, jiggling her keys, and Peter would grab her hand. She could see all of the ex-bulimics and soon-to-be Valium addicts hunched over their computers. Of course they had computers. They were always asking too much, always wanting something. Coming back to the 'servant's quarters' after her fever, Cleo could feel the plumbing breaking, and Emma floating away in her hallucination.

"Emma," Cleo cried, "Dammit, come back, come to my party." And there she was, sitting by the river, looking at Cleo's hands and saying, "Look pretty clean to me."

33

Lying on her futon, Cleo remembered North Mills again. This time, she remembered that it was cold again, the way that it got in the Notch between Connecticut and Massachusetts, and she recalled that the cracks in the house would let the air in. She thought about how they would tack up old blankets and plug in heaters, but the cold never stopped. Those blankets were so old; displaying the fraying name of 'Hartford Hospital'. The current nightmare Cleo had was about being half way between home and school on the freezing street, with no bus change. In the dream, the icy rocks of the cars whizzing by were hitting her, and she was stumbling, her feet shuffling. Beginning to lose feeling, her fingers felt like giants in their thin gloves. She felt her ears, every part of her, vulnerable and open to the elements. Then, she recalled having lain down in the white, white snow bank. She was ready, really warm, knowing it was time to leave.

Cleo stumbled over to Fountain Avenue, wringing her sweaty hands as she walked over the hill. She saw the first fallen snow of winter, slushy again and Cleo nearly slipped. She entered the home of the drummers. It struck her immediately. She saw posters carefully pasted up by Ed LeBlanc. Next to those John Coltrane posters, she saw posters of the great African Kings and Queens. She noticed the Queen of Sheba, her beautiful countenance struck Cleo immediately. Niema and Cleo stumbled upstairs to the room with clothes strewn about, past Harold and the heavy metal drumming. Cleo thought of the Professor and wondered where he would be now. He had pronounced things differently than Bob, and Bob told Cleo that he had the details of his studies wrong. Bob was always telling Cleo that she belonged at Middlesex, that she was "just as good as them," but the Professor had subtle put-downs. Bob finally told Cleo that the names of the Professor's sports teams at prep school were wrong. The Professor always invited Cleo to this house or that house for dinners or discussions. Bob said that some people used their positions for control. Cleo thought that the Professor cared.

"When my father used to take me to the Somerset Club, we would always enjoy a fine cocktail," the Professor said, "he enjoyed vodka." Bob said that that was not the drink of choice at the Somerset Club. The Professor said that 'his people' liked to drink.

"You know that they are having a dinner at the Asia house tonight?" Cleo said to Niema. "I was going to call my mother, not that she would go..." There seemed to be specific rules for each group, and Bob certainly knew his rules, much better than the Professor knew his. "But I don't speak Japanese, or look Japanese...Jeff is going to something called Shabbat, but I don't know what that is," she said.

"Well, they don't speak Black at the Malcolm X house, so I'm not going...my Dad caught me with some lines today, he didn't say anything..." Niema said.

"He never says anything," Cleo said. Niema smoked into yellowing pillows, to keep the smoke from wafting into the house.

"Don't worry, your mom won't know you are doing this in the house," Cleo said. "She trusts me, I am in school, you know..."

"I'm really aware of that and you better stay there...She DOES trust you," said Niema. She looked over and added, "They want my dad at the Malcolm X house, to play."

After more types of substance abuse, Cleo replied, "Jesus Christ, they have houses for everything...fucking everything."

"Houses of detention," Niema said, "Those kids have not even listened to the whole Malcolm X speech, and they just like the gun image." They fell down; looking for something, trembling. The beating of Harold's drums reverberated upstairs. Cleo wanted more than ever to speak Japanese then, Japanese with an original accent; and she wanted to speak the other language of her other side, whatever that was. Bob loved her so much and believed in her, but somehow, it was not enough. Cleo took up the pipe.

34

It was 5 a.m., and Cleo was still coming down. At 7:00 she had to go to Somers State Prison to bring Niema to see Johnny, now her ex-boyfriend, who had been put away for gun charges. She borrowed a car from one of the people Niema knew. She thought she could use a line to get up, but there was not one. It was eerie as they drove by Hartford in the low-riding Cadillac. The clouds in the sky were many graded, like the circular cymbals, driving through the drizzle that seemed to patter in rhythm. Cleo kept crossing the centerline of I-84, and Niema had to grab the wheel from her to navigate them back on course. They drove past the iridescent fields to the compound. Cleo pulled right in.

"Aren't these the employee spaces?" Niema asked.

"My Dad worked here years ago," Cleo said. She pulled the car into the space with precision. Cleo seemed to know how to pull into prisons. Her father had worked at Somers when prison gangs were just beginning, when La Neta was in its nascence.

"Of course, he could never keep a job," Cleo mumbled. They walked into the building, with its barbed wire and tower, a state institution like the DMV with bars. Cleo sat in the waiting room, at home almost, doing her homework as a guard led shackled youth in grey clothing by her.

"Fish will be biting pretty good up at the lake this spring," one guard said.

"Yep, I just bought me a new rod and reel," replied the other guard, who was checking another prisoner in. Cleo continued with her reading and underlining, thinking about her mother and father, about fathers and mothers and silence, lack of language. As she sat at the prison, Cleo thought of Harold and his picture of the dragon and the eggs – the eggs, the carefully crafted lines and words. Cleo thought of the way he treated her like a celebrity. She thought of his arms; his bulging, uneven muscles in his half T-shirt. She felt electric all over in the seat, thinking of the Super continent and its music. But it was not sexual. On some level, the LeBlancs read minds. Bob sometimes came to meet Niema at the house on Fountain Avenue, and Ed came out on the porch. Ed and Bob might chat about the weather, but it was not about the clouds. They communicated spiritually. "He read right through me," Bob said. They were all connected like the seasons.

35

Niema and Cleo stumbled into the LeBlanc's house. Rolling upstairs, they listened to Harold's incantations. He was practicing some softer variations.

"Fucking Johnny's a loser," he said, as they rounded the stairs. "You guys are really starting to embarrass us," he said and kept on drumming. Cleo knew that Harold's father had toured Morocco and Africa in the 1960s. The sounds that day felt North African.

"He should talk," Niema said. Cleo noticed the short, pale figure, the tight ringlets of hair circling her forehead, accenting her Choctaw nose. She also knew that they went to see Johnny; she had given them the money for gas. She always helped them with the basics. Cleo panicked. She remembered that she had scheduled an appointment with the Professor last week. Bob was sleeping in her room. She gathered her jean jacket, ran downstairs over the hill, past the package store, and she stopped, panting, at the door of the department.

"Sit down," the Professor pointed at the chair. He put his book on the desk. "You have to write about reciprocity," he said, "it's an easy concept to grasp…for instance, if a guy gives you a picture… and you give him…" Cleo stared at a map on the wall. "You give him something of yours…"

"I think, I think," Cleo was still breathing heavily, "It has to do with life crisis rites," the Professor told her, "Life crisis rights, you know."

"You are right, but you need a more complicated analysis than the one I read in your paper. Add in some history and law." Clenching his teeth, he further continued, "When I was a child in, uh, Beverly, I attended Shore County Day School and I learned Greek and Latin and everything that was essential to a good education…and that is what I am trying to teach you."

"You can't teach me SHIT…YOU can't tell ME how to define selfhood," Cleo yelled and ran out, down the steps towards the Victorian. "And Robert Treat Paine told me you were not in any of Shore County's classes, he still gets the alumni notes!" As Cleo ran, she could barely hear the Professor sob. That weekend, Bob had taught her the word '*nouveau riche*'. Bob could never fit in as a part of any faculty, but he knew the vocabulary. The good professors, like Cooper, Davison, and even the 'visiting Buddhism prof' O'Malley encouraged her, supported her, and made her feel included. But Cleo was still missing something. She went back to the Victorian, comforted to see Emma, who was cleaning up bottles of scotch. Cleo's birthday was approaching. She had been thinking about a party for weeks. She had another version of a paper due, there was a grant proposal, and someone called Emily was talking to someone named Jonathan about their cottage on Martha's Vineyard. Cleo wanted to see Peter, but Peter had gone to the family estate in Jamestown, New York, leaving behind his huge traffic light. Cleo could plug the light in and get any color that she wanted. She called up Niema. "There's a fuckin' traffic light here, a fuckin' traffic light, nothing better for my birthday…sister, I need some junk…you know where I can get some junk? You understand, I have got that emptiness in my head again…"

"Do your papers," Niema said.

"I needed something, please," Cleo pleaded.

"No," she firmly replied. Cleo knew that Niema knew where the 'stuff' was. They had been to the apartments the other day. "No way, sister…I don't know ANYONE in this town that got that…you aint got works, anyway. What you gonna do, snort the stuff?" Cleo stood there, shaking.

"I'm tired of that…I got works, it's my birthday."

"I'll kill those kids…they gave it to you, didn't they?"

"Fucking help me." Cleo said.

"Look, thanks for taking me to see Johnny, but I don't know no one…look, take care of yourself, you know we love you," Niema said.

"I love you guys, too," Cleo said.

"Then come over," she said. She put the receiver of the payphone down, the back of her head screaming with unforeseen heat. She went over the hill past the package store again. She knew there were many odd medical implements at the Victorian. People's parents were doctors and owned medical supply companies. Everything was easy to get at the Victorian; everything but Cleo's place and time in life. Niema came down the stairs at the Fountain Avenue house with the same pained look as her mother; her brow like the posters pasted against the wall, wrinkled with fine furrows. "I know it's your birthday, Daddy's playing in Atlanta this weekend…I want you to come, it's a festival in his honor…kinda funny, it's on your birthday," Niema said.

"Yeah, kinda funny, I don't know, I am not feeling that good," Cleo said.

"Harold's going. The whole family is going, come with us." Cleo knew that Ed LeBlanc was not well, and that this might be the last chance to see him perform. She lay down on the red couch with a fever, but replied, "I'll go." Cleo felt the emptiness from the racial taunts of childhood, to the freezing cold, to the intellectual wasteland of North Mills. Sometimes, Bob would hold her for hours as she shook and shook, unable to stop. Cleo would also wake upright from sleep, holding her hands above her body against blows from her past. Bob whispered to her and stroked her hair. They listened to Tom Waits and Richard Thompson; the two artist's deep lyrics holding them together. But Bob refused to baby her. Cleo had to feel the music.

36

Like the rivers of the South, the Savannah and the Mississippi, Cleo was raging and seething, turning twenty-one, head singing as the plane set down. The taxi took her to the heart of the city. She had not taken a taxi that way before, to an event, and she did not know what to say when she got into that yellow taxi. The air felt like a warm, melon-colored blanket around her as she stepped carefully into the seat. Her lips were red and full and her flowered dress clung to her with her restrung pearls about her throat. Arriving at the High Museum of Art on Peachtree Street, she met Niema; that night, a daughter for whom any father would have shot a man in cold blood…Niema was carefully, nervously walking in the spacious outer area of the hall. She popped out and said, "Lumita, Ma, its Lumita, she is here; Harold, Daddy, its Lumita."

Ed raised his eyebrows, cracked an indecipherable smile. "I don't know any Lumita," he said. Cleo embraced Niema, as she had on the third seat of the Greyhound to New York, and watched all the musicians gather together that night in tribute to the father, she knew, that was not long for this world. She felt a feeling of elevation as the people packed the hall, the family and friends of the performers who had flown in from New Orleans and the cities of the South. The simple spoken words brought with them flying clouds of air. They were coming together after so many years. Sagittarius Jackson was flying in from Europe to meet his roommate from New Orleans, Ed LeBlanc. As the Professor had mentioned, it was the Sagittarius Jackson Quartet – Sagittarius Jackson, Delbert Redbone, Don Channing, and Ed LeBlanc. People were crowding the hall, standing outside, as there was no room left in the auditorium.

"Sit up here," Mrs. LeBlanc said. The lights dimmed that Atlanta evening, and the show began. At first, the hall was completely silent, with not an audible sound. Then, he began to play, and it was as if there was no beginning; the lightning fast way he calculated the rhythm, within the structure, yet flying. He was still the silent man from the rickety house, but on stage, he was a different man. LeBlanc followed the other players in an odd way; but he was undeniably himself, undeniably the man behind the sunglasses that most of the college faculty did not understand. Men that Cleo knew at Middlesex were always full of talk, all of those future businessman with a line, and professors with a thousand words. She remembered from her studies, "Selfhood, the ceremony of transfer. The mechanisms of obligation that are resident in the gifts themselves." He had no words, this man had not a single word, just the instrument, the way the cymbal resonated along with Sagittarius Jackson's saxophone line – it was like the waves inside her. The soft tapping brought those waves out gently.

Blue, blue, blue, all the blues the man had ever seen came to life – the Pacific of the Monterrey Bay, the Mediterranean, the Straits of Gibraltar – that space between Europe and Africa, and the waters off the coast of Morocco. These were the places Cleo had yet to see, but he could bring to her. He materialized other colors too, with the veiled sunset that touches upon the silent desert and the many-hued hills of Northern Africa; greens, golds, and blues, were illuminated in the fading light. He showed Cleo Morocco's ancient rhythms shifting with the wrinkles of sand appearing from faceless men ladling soup into bowls at 3 a.m. and she smiled as the hooked noses sniffed the scent of the mountain's menses. The drum was like the taste of atlas wine; dark and mysterious. He was laughing with open mouth, creating the sounds, the sounds of distance. He brought to Cleo the cities, the sea, those mountains; the face of a different continent. He could make a feeling of softness and a feeling of fury with that cymbal. He was the old man with quiet moves. Sagittarius was smiling as he took out his left-handed violin. He smiled at Ed and the air softened. This was the music of the streets of America, the mountains of Morocco, and of the African Kings and Queens. It was a music that transcended halfness and difference. Cleo thought of those layered clouds on the way to Somers State Prison, and of her boxer father and Japanese mother. Then they played 'free form jazz', the kind of jazz that has been highly criticized for its lack of structure. But it had its own unique and original style. Cleo was petrified...petrified that this music could carry her places. Niema, Harold and Cleo watched the man, the musician, eyes deep in his sockets. Ed had barely spoken in the crowded backstage area that they had huddled in before the concert, but would occasionally cough or smile. Cleo remembered his staring, coughing, staring at the floorboards, smoking a cigarette in the house up North. She remembered sensing death, and seeing the Queen of Sheba on the wall. She shook, afraid.

They played together as that quartet. That evening the family played life music sweet and strong, free form. Niema was that saxophone, that wailing intense strength; that bayou magic Native, and the practiced color. Cleo swayed and her eyes turned different, almost liquid. Harry was that drum, of course, that followed. Then Delbert Redbone played his instrument, like the mother, the stand-up bass; soft stringed instruments of consciousness. They were steady, as carmel earth waits for spring and sprouts life from white. They were low-flying birds not touching the breathing land, but moving in harmony with it. Cleo remembered Mrs. LeBlanc greeting them, tired, watching them come from New York City and prison. Ed loved and followed the bass like her simple, quiet way. Then, Don Channing wailed on his short horn and the beads of sweat came down his face. Cleo saw his hair that stood out in dreads on his head. She remembered how he had brought Niema an imported beer from Europe. Like Cleo, drunk with it all, he played. Making the body and drums one, Ed followed Don, whose kids had grown up with his children. His offspring were now movie stars and musicians. Channing, too, was, like the sound, on its way down into the ground, the earth. Family – not like clubs, smoky, mystic, drowning, but more stable, less swift and dark. The family was always there, the heavy metal musician and the leopard skin dancer – the bass, the saxophone, the horn, and finally, the drums.

Cleo watched that family on a warm night in Atlanta. Like the shooting up sensation in the chocolate brown vein, the color of blood was the same, coming together. The sound in the hall shifted and she watched him move with the instrument, not looking at the crowd from his dark glasses. She had heard jazz before, but now the essence of the music became story for her; the eddies of consciousness. She had that feeling that she was being let into something privileged to share the blood ocean with the mystic masters. The weeping willows swept the banks of the muddy rivers, and she watched the rooms passing by his eyes – the one he had shared with Sagittarius Jackson; California, Africa, New York City; Music – nodding, waiting, flying and dancing. Cleo also thought of Emma's pain, of her quiet acceptance, and her furious, intense cleaning. She sat with the family in the front row. Cleo felt the Savannah River like honey lips on the saxophone. It was a mystery to her, the way he followed, yet lead, the way that man could make the cymbals move. Sliding down in her seat, holding her arm, she was not looking at the crowd, but inside, to that 'essential element'. The barge with the cargo navigated to the dock, and she knew that she had never been so close to anyone, to anything, as she had been recently.

Cleo had always been embarrassed about her own splintered way of living, those silent birthdays, but that evening, she knew where the levels came from; they came from the currents in the water, the earth, and the air; those levels sustained, they maintained, juxtaposed with life and freedom, sending her somewhere. At the end, the quartet embraced with a love; the kind of love that goes into a child's lullaby. The jazz was a more complex music than anything she had ever heard; no simple lines, no words. That night, the man whose eyes pierced her smiled, he was doing what he enjoyed most, communicating with those that understood. The cheap wine hangover beat into Cleo's head. She looked over to the sad-eyed woman and her dark-skinned daughter and son in a leather jacket. She realized that she was trying to fight back with white rocks thrown at enemies, who named the words, who defined the space where she lived and worked. She knew now, there was a better addiction.

As they waited after the concert, Mrs. LeBlanc said, "You're a survivor, Lumita, just remember that." Stumbling around the hotel bar to the street with Niema, the beautiful soul in a black miniskirt, drinking tequila and eating chicken, she realized that she would make it through. She wasn't going to get out of the partying scene right away, but would manage to manage it. On that warm Southern night, the man and his music, the family brought Cleo through. One concert, fifteen years, a shell was broken, a growth had begun. Cleo could make it through the lectures at school in time to see Bob, she could talk to the Professor, and she could leave Emma a beer. She knew what self was, and its definition.

37

Bob took Cleo to Montreal on the train. The train rolled through the early winter over the tracks at night through White River Junction, past the old New England working class towns that were farther from cities than North Mills. They cuddled next to each other as the train crossed into another country. No one needed passports in 1987. Cleo awoke to a city with cobblestone streets and bars open all night, serving Labatt's beer at 8 a.m. Cathedrals peaked up into the cold air. Cleo's old green down jacket warmed her as did Bob's hand holding hers. They walked through the city. The Montreal Forum boomed with the cheering sounds. They sat down and Rob drank his beer and smiled slightly. The sound of the skates across ice reminded Cleo of a movie she had seen about the chariot races and lion fights in Rome. They were close enough to the penalty box to hear the curses and smell the sweat. Then, the bodies hit the side of the rink…blood spurted out…the crowd roared and the clink of beer bottles on the ice rang in Cleo's ears. Bob secretly rooted for the Bruins, but enjoyed the Canadien's gaols. The French rolled off his tongue like fine liquor.

After the game, they stayed up all night in a bar that played 70s music. The clientele wore their hair like the front cover of rock albums and the conversation was gentle, as if the 1980s had not arrived. But as the sun rose, Cleo and Bob headed to the train station, boarded the southbound train, and immediately fell asleep in their seats. When they awoke, they were in Buffalo. The snow was falling heavily and the wind was kicking up against the train station. The city was shut down for the night, and they realized that they had to run, in below zero weather, to catch the Greyhound bus to Springfield.

"The last bus has left," the station agent said.

"But, but we have tickets," Cleo pleaded. The agent lowered the metal covering of the window. It screeched uncomfortably.

"Try to get a taxi to a hotel." Cleo and Bob saw the last taxi idling in the lot. They raced across the icy ground to hail him. The ice was making the road slick as the driver took Bob to the ATM at the bank.

"Farmer's and Mechanics does not have an agreement with..." Cleo clenched. The driver let them back in and they stopped at several hotels, with neon signs fizzing on and off...

"Sorry, cold night, convention in town..." Bob and Cleo looked at each other.

The driver said, "I will take you back to the station, but it's closing." They slid into the station, which indeed was getting ready to close.

"Sir...sir," Bob said.

"We are closing..."

"But we purchased these tickets..." The bums grabbed their blankets and hobbled off to find heat.

"Well, try Peter Pan..." The taxi was leaving, but they ran after it, bags in tow.

"You again," the driver sneered. "P...Peter Pan," He drove them a few blocks away...Cleo saw the green and white bus starting to pull out. They bumbled out of the taxi in the cold and ran. The driver stopped, opened the door, and looked down, his uniform rumpled and his eyes tired.

Cleo raised their tickets up. She got on the first step.

"Those are Greyhound..." the driver said, as passengers began rubbing themselves from the cold...

"Please, please..."

"Get in," he said. "We stopped that agreement with them a while back, but just get in." Bob and Cleo jumped up the steps into the warmth, once again.

38

Bob knew that in North Mills, Cleo had been isolated and unable to move. When they got home from the other country, Bob gave Cleo $700 and Henry Rawinger took Cleo to his mechanic in Middleton who had a car – a mustard colored 78 Plymouth Fury. She began to cope with the adult activities of emissions, insurance, and license plates. The Middleton garage was comforting like the fields. There was grease, tools, and a smell that did not waft up to Middlesex. The guys were like her friends from the tobacco fields, but, somehow, now, she had trouble 'talking the talk.'

"We need to adjust the intake," the mechanic said. Cleo was thinking about theoretical physics and she looked blankly at the man with his grizzled face and thinning hair.

"That will be eighty dollars," he said. Cleo felt herself clench up. She wrote one of her first checks and watched the mechanic's hands enter the body of her new steed.

Cleo heard the sound of the crash; the abrupt end of youth. The City of Northampton parking meter wobbled. "Let's go to breakfast," Bob said, cracking a smile. Cleo looked up at the awning of the restaurant, with its red and white stripes. The police lights pulsed and the radio crackled. Bob came out and talked to the officer. It was as if nothing happened. Breakfast usually took three hours; with coffee, bagels, and eggs. Bob read the paper as always and commented on world events. That day, he was talking about Oliver North and how he was a 'small potato.' Bob smiled, "As Edmund Burke said, Patriotism is the last bastion of the scoundrel."

Cleo repeated Burke's phrase in North Mills as her parents looked out at her new car. The old handmade house with its many sculptures seemed like a toy home to Cleo, not a place she had actually lived. Cleo's stooped over father wore a worn brown cardigan with elbow patches.

"At least you got an American made car," he said, wiping his glasses with an old, yellowed handkerchief, something that Cleo had found so embarrassing in high school. Now, she did not care.

"Let's go to Chinese," her small mother said, "I have money from teaching Japanese." They walked down the stone steps, got into the big mustard colored car and headed up the hills into Canton. Cleo savored the tea at the only Asian restaurant within 30 miles of her mother's house. They said very few words that day, but they looked at each other, finally looked at each other. Cleo's mom paid for lunch and said, "You can't take it with you."

39

Bob was down for the weekend and Henry, Peter, and Jeff were clowning around on the top of the Plymouth. Peter was pointing to the interior of the car, "Look, it's a Plymouth Fury Salon," he laughed. Bob and Cleo were hanging around in the room with people dropping in and out. Paige Meyerson popped in. She was the daughter of attorney Meyerson, owner of one of the first low cost law firms in the US. She was just back from Thailand and was talking to Bob and Cleo about attending the 'Lesbian, Bisexual, and Questioning' group. "Look, I was just questioning," she said. "And well, they weren't very understanding." We talked about her father's philosophy of low cost law firms, making the law affordable to others, accident victims and the like. Susannah Goodrich also came by. Her father was famous Princeton economist whose editor at *New York* Magazine had renamed him 'Maynard Keynes'. Susannah's father had been the editor of the 'Harvard Crimson' and was also a Rhodes scholar. He wrote the books The Money Works and The Roaring Economies, which they were in the middle of. He also wrote the screenplay for a movie with James Garner (Cleo's childhood hero) and Lee Remick. He would soon be rubbing elbows with Warren Buffet and Gorbachev and would be featured in Nissan commercials. But his daughter, like Paige Meyerson, just wanted to make a difference. It was one of those days when everybody was dropping by. Mary was coming by from visiting 'The Ugly House', whose residents liked science fiction and the new Cons, or science fiction conventions that were emerging, Lurch, named after the character in the Addams family, walked by.

He wore a long, black cape and it was flowing in the crisp air.

Mary, Ed, Bob, and Cleo were all listening to the Fairport Convention, and Mary was getting freaked out by Sandy Denny's song, 'Meet on the Ledge'. That day, Mary did a 'past life' reading with Jeff and Cleo and she was also going to do a tarot reading. In the 'past life' reading, Mary and Jeff said that Cleo's face turned into the face of a Chinese man from the 1800s. They saw the man sitting behind a money cage, counting. The message, they said, was that Cleo should not live for money, or else she would end up unhappy like that money counter. Cleo couldn't recall what Jeff and Mary were in their past lives. Their present life was weird enough. Bob and Ed left for Cleo's room to talk about the latest issue of *The Nation*. Mary then placed the cards on the living room table. Cleo saw the Queens, the Cups, and the Magicians, which gave her a feeling of being transported back to a time that Mary costumed – the elaborate sorcerer's outfits, the knights, and the Queens and their Court. Cleo felt, however, that this time period was not for her.

She was beginning to realize that her skin had a different pigment. No one was going to put her in any Court, unless she was clearing the dishes, as she was doing at Middlesex. All those Ugly House people could go back into a time where they could decide their own role in the world, because their role in present time was already set. It was all for naught, anyway; Mary refused to tell her what she found in Cleo's cards. Earlier, there had been a male threesome in the Cobb House and the men were walking down the street, smiling. Cleo thought that she had seen the house ghost, but it was just these men. It felt like a different time; perhaps it was Greece or Rome. The Victorian had its own past lives, tarot, and something off of a painting in a Greek urn happening almost every day. Cleo opened the letter that was sitting on her desk.

Dear Lumita,

Your mother and I went to the doctor and your mother has been diagnosed with colon cancer. She has a 50/50 chance to live...

Cleo read the rest of the letter. Her mother was old, but she seemed to stay the same age the entire time that she was grew up. Cleo had thought that her Dad, who was always complaining like Fred Sanford, would be the one to die. But their food was often old and even expired. The meat was a thin cut and yellowing. Cleo's mom always took the oldest bits. It stuck in her colon, the food and the life.

"My mom is dying," Cleo said to Bob, who was lying on the futon.

"I know," he said. Mary later told Cleo that, at the tarot reading, she had pulled out the death card. The cards always had a bad timing for Cleo, it seemed. She knew that she needed to go on to do something, 'but what?' She wondered.

Anne Greenbaum was head of the Writing Program at Middlesex, and her husband was a dean. There were very few writing classes at the university, but since Cleo was a senior she was able to enroll in her small workshop. Cleo put pen to paper. The words just came because she felt that the world she knew needed to be cataloged because it was disappearing. A fellow student, Joanna Greenberg, read Cleo's papers. Joanna wore a lumberjack check shirt and combat boots. Her brown, curly hair fell over her shoulders. Cleo read Joanna's work as well.

I looked at the certificate that fell out of the card; it was from Greenwich plastic surgeons...my mother looked at me as I held the birthday card. She was smiling. She said, "Your nose can look like a model's..."

"Wow, rich people suffer, too," Cleo said. "My mom would never do that to me, even if she had money." Joanna put her paper down.

"Your suffering is clear, too. This is not undergraduate level writing," she said. "This is something else…" Cleo was shocked. Anne Greenbaum smiled. The class progressed and Cleo continued to write about issues that she had tried to bring up in her 'Towards a Socialist America' class. But no one in those classes wanted to hear about or visit the places Cleo wrote about. In Greenbaum's class, Cleo found a voice and the place for it.

40

The last year at Middlesex, 1988, Cleo lived between the cities of Northampton and Middleton, taking the Plymouth Fury up I-91, or, sometimes, surreptitiously, up the back roads she had traveled with her parents. But the Bay State SRO was getting old. The bed was small and people left *Penthouse* and *Hustler* magazines in the bathroom. Finally, Bob rented a room in a rooming house across the street from Amherst College.

That weekend that they moved to Amherst, Bob introduced Cleo to Ingmar Bergman. On the small TV that was connected to a black cable box, they watched *The Seventh Seal* and also Bertolucci's *Last Tango in Paris*. When they were not having fun outside, they explored the intensity of foreign cinema, Kate Wolf's folk music and the work of Toni Morrison and Borges. They went to the fancy Northampton Hotel for drinks, ate in nice country restaurants in Florence, and frequented ethnic restaurants all over the Pioneer Valley. The day before they went to a new Moroccan restaurant, Cleo learned to eat with her hands. They watched Larry Holmes boxing on the big TV at the bar and, later in the night, watched Antonini movies in the room. Cleo's heart, stomach, and mind were full.

41

Cleo first met Maddog at the American Legion, Post #76, on a side street near Amherst College. Bob had taken her there for cheap drinks and to watch football. She was learning how to bet. Cleo had never been to an American legion before. In fact, she had a sort of negative attitude toward them. This Legion, however, was different. Across from the old hotel which was converted into a Senior Citizens home, it was part of the local bar scene and had welcomed 'townies' for years. That Sunday, in front of Ethel, the comfortably seated Black bartender, Cleo was introduced to John Maddigan.

"This is Maddog," Bob said. Maddog stood about five-foot-six and was paper-thin.

"John Maddigan, please," said the man. "A little respect. There are ladies present." And so Cleo sat next to John Maddigan at the short bar and Bob ordered her a Budweiser. Ethel eyed Cleo, a woman barely old enough to drink.

"I can't believe that you are still alive, Maddog," Bob said. "You look a lot better than when I last saw you." Bob was gone from the scene for years and was reacquainting himself with the old crowd.

"I got new blood in me," said John. He quickly changed the subject. "Bob and I go back a long time…he never hung out much with women, he was always with us, shooting pool, causing trouble… and he ran that bar at Hampshire College…of course, I won't tell you about that."

"My knee still aches from that night," Bob said. Bob had nearly given his father a mild stroke by not applying to Harvard and enrolling in experimental Hampshire College. His father's fears, however, had been assuaged when he discovered that his son could indeed do business deals of many kinds. But Bob, although considered an alum of Hampshire, had never actually graduated from the school. He had given up on selling things and running businesses.

"I remember the look on your old man's face when I showed up in 'Frisco, it was at the Great White Buffalo's' place. I had gotten in a fight that night, and Bob picks up the blanket on the couch he'd been sleeping on…there I am, three thousand miles later, bleeding on his couch…we had some wild times out there."

"Like the time you had the ass ripped outta your pants and you were shooting pool on Sixth Street at six in the morning…you didn't even know it," Bob said.

"Please," said John, "but, seriously, forget all of those stories. This is the first time I seen this guy serious." He hesitated. "…And I'm glad you're taking him away from all this…say, you want to see my tattoos?"

"Uh, sure," Cleo said, thinking that his stick arms were quite amazing. John then lifted up his white T-shirt to his shoulders and turned his back to her. Cleo was introduced to the dragon and the lady, and the spirals and the loops of blue-green that were history on the back of this paper board man.

"Goddamn," Cleo said loudly. Ethel stared her wickedest stare and Cleo turned red. She realized that this was, after all, the American Legion, and she was a guest. That's how she would always remember Maddog – pulling up his shirt and showing her his tattoos in the American Legion. He was like that, quick with his actions. In an incident in the hotel across the street, he had slit the throat of a guy who had wronged him and spent some time in prison. There was too much wine, and a quick wrist, but it was, luckily, not a fatal incident. At first, when Maddog started coming over, Cleo had told Bob that she did not like him. She had nothing in common with him. He was the local 'homeless' drunk who had spent a lot of time in jail and never seemed to set his life straight, and Cleo was a student at a private college who enjoyed reading the great philosophers. She had come to resent the way Maddog came by late at night to talk to Bob, and when he fell asleep on the couch, how those dragon tattoos would stand out on his sticklike arms as he wasn't eating enough. But Cleo got used to Maddog.

The man became a fixture in their lives over the year, sleeping occasionally in the bushes by their place on Pleasant Street with Gary Nelson, who had moved back East, and Jimmy Brown, who worked pouring concrete. Gary was welcomed at the VFW, of course. They were quite a scene on a Saturday morning, with their large size matching ALF T-shirts that Jimmy had purchased from the Ames department store in the mall. Maddog, Jimmy, and Gary had their little cave in the bushes. There was an occasional cherry brandy bottle left there, but most of the time it was clean. They respected the bushes. Like gardeners, they tended to their little spot. Maddog would pop out of the bushes in the morning with a little smile. Before Cleo's graduation, he would often say to Cleo, "When are we going to see the piece of paper?"

"Sometime soon," she promised, smiling.

"Well, I wanna see it when you're done, promise?" Cleo promised.

He would ask regularly, as he tended the bushes, about her progress. Cleo carried her books past him and smiled. Maddog always surprised her. One night, 'Hush…Hush Sweet Charlotte' with Bette Davis was on cable television, and Cleo managed to scare herself half to death watching the movie until 2 a.m. in the morning. She walked out of the bathroom in the hall with a certain amount of trepidation. She saw a body. "Oh, my God." She looked. "It couldn't be? Maddog."

He wasn't moving, either. She screamed. She reached down to touch him. He didn't move. Then she heard it; the snore that was almost a laugh. He was sleeping soundly. She was glad that he was alive.

Then there were the stains on the stairs. Maddog knew that Cleo had stayed up days on end at Middlesex, working on her Senior Essay. She holed up in the garret of the anthropology building, allowing no one to visit. Cleo saw Jeff circling the block in his VW microbus, over and over, hoping to get Cleo's attention over some crisis. But the door was locked and Cleo was not sleeping. She was working. Maddog also knew that Cleo had limited time with Bob on weekends, and she would get mad at him for keeping 'the old man' up. Maddog began leaving espresso and muffins and flowers at the door for breakfasts. He recently began working at one of the colleges as a janitor, and you know what that meant – keys, all sorts of keys. The interesting thing about the escapades was that no one caught him. Coffee was free for employees and the muffins had not been sold, so why let them go to waste? The bosses knew he did it, and they let him get away with it. He brought back gum, candy, and throat lozenges. One day, he came back with twenty packages of Celestial Seasonings teas, likely left over from some banquet. He would also bring rows and rows of scratch off lottery tickets. Cleo and Maddog took enormous pleasure in scratching off fifty tickets at a time, gleefully rubbing the silver surface with their nickels. They never said anything when they cashed them in. It got out of hand, however, when he brought things from the freezer. There was a trail of ice cream all the way from the college, up the stairs, and into the apartment.

"I knew you were studying for finals." He grinned. "Ben and Jerry's." Sometimes Cleo would be heading back to Middlesex at 5 a.m. and she would notice a form on the bench as the mist rolled through the valley. He was curled up in a ball on Main Street across from the cop shop and the village green and the church. But the Amherst PD let him stay there. Maddog also often slept in the local cemetery where Emily Dickinson is buried. It was peaceful, he said, especially during the day. Cleo would visit him there before her classes. Then, on hot days, they went up to the Cushman Country Store, where he had a job on and off taking the six-pack rings off the six packs in the cooler. He cut up some cold cuts, they would have some cold ones, and they would head for Silver Bridge. Cleo would spend the afternoon with Maddog, Bob, Gary, and Jimmy Brown, with their feet in the water, enjoying the afternoon sunshine.

Frank from the Santa Cruz Cal Force office, quit fundraising and was working selling rolling tobacco at Augie's on Main Street. He had seen 500 Grateful Dead shows and was following the tour when he could. Bob and Cleo went over to his apartment where his roommates Jeanne Moultine and Marsha were hanging out. Jeanne, an ex-union organizer was listening to Pharoah Sanders when Cleo and Bob walked in to the kitchen of the Victorian.

"I hear you were a union organizer," Bob said.

"I worked in a factory in Michigan where the conditions were horrible," Jeanie said, raising a Rolling Rock. "I organized the people to protest to change the conditions."

"Wow," Bob said. Jeanne's hair was spiked up with gel and she had a rose tattoo on her wrist. Cleo knew no Middlesex students who had worked in factories.

"Was your family supportive?" Cleo asked Jeanne.

"My father left the family at age seven and mom had died in a car accident when I was thirteen. Dad left with a waitress named Jeanie, believe it or not," she said.

"I'm sorry," Cleo said. "I worked tobacco and my Dad is a conspiracy theorist."

Cleo and Bob often visited the apartment and became better friends with Jeanne than with Frank, who was eventually kicked out of the apartment. He was replaced by M.B., a heroin addict, whose Dad was in the mob. It was a world of people with no parents, parents who were distant or engaged in mob activities. It was their own family of outsiders. Peter Fivecoats wondered why Cleo was not at Middlesex. It was hard to explain to him.

The day Cleo finished her last exam, she headed out to Amherst. The class was called 'The Civil Rights Movement' and was taught by a white Professor from Yale. Cleo thought he was fake, but when she wrote her last line for Middlesex, she knew that she would not be dealing with his ilk for a long time. There was a slight breeze and some rain that last day. Cleo drove the Plymouth steadily up the highway watching the tobacco fields and the insurance companies go by. She picked up Bob.

"Congratulations, Lumita Cleopatra Izumi Sugarman," he smiled, putting his hand on hers. "Pull in here." The old tents pulsed with sound. The carnival located between Northampton and Amherst seemed as if it was situated in Eastern Europe, in a dusty town far away. Cleo saw the old, stately houses disappear as they pulled into the open field. A variety of townies in old cars pulled in, taking out cheap baby carriages that looked like old arm slings. The women had put on hairspray and the men had tattoos. Cleo queued for the small, rickety rides run by men with grizzled faces. As those cages whirled around, and Bob watched Cleo from below, she felt that she could see out to Asia. Her feet dangled, the drops of rain hit her, and she smiled the broad smile of a child. The cages swung, and Cleo felt a sensation of movement and buoyancy. Right after, Bob led Cleo to see all the acts under the Big Top. She reached out to the clown, whose smile was as wide as Massachusetts, and hugged him. Bob took her picture with the man with a clown nose and huge, white lips, completing the Felliniesque carnival, and leading on to the next circus.

Right before Cleo graduated, Maddog came up to her one day at the river and said, “I have a present for you.” He handed her a small package. Cleo opened the crisp paper. She pulled out a triangle-shaped pendant with a turquoise moon on it. “I figure you could put it on a necklace or something,” Maddog said slowly. Somehow, Cleo knew that Maddog had not stolen this gift and she had no words for that moment. It wasn’t that the used toolset for her Plymouth that her family had given her in a crumpled Bonwit Teller bag wasn’t appropriate; she knew, however, that Bonwit Teller did not sell toolsets. The necklace was a true gift. Maddog was also the one who had a pig roast for her.

“We have to celebrate,” he said. “Somebody’s gotta have a party for you.” Cleo watched the pig spin with Maddog and Bob and Gary and Jimmy. It was better than the president of the college’s cocktail party, where the Director of Public Safety had tried to manhandle Bob. Cleo, needless to say, had to intervene. They had arrived at the president’s party with twelve packs of Milwaukie’s Best. Bob, whose family had owned many houses like the Middlesex presidents, just laughed. Cleo did not realize it was not BYOB, and did not want to make the same mistake she had with her first pot luck at Middlesex. Staring at the columns of the President’s house, a mother was saying to her graduate, “It’s just as I pictured it, the warm, gentle breeze under the ionic columns.” Bob, right next to her, burst out laughing, and said through clenched teeth in his best WASP way.

“It’s Juh-ust as I pick-turedittt…the wahm gentle breeze undahh the iiioniccc columns,” he said. The mother stared at him. Cleo laughed and offered her a Milwaukie’s Best.

“This is a college educated woman,” Maddog said, smiling, as they hung out at her real party, He went on to tell the whole town about how Cleo was graduating. She stopped being vegetarian for the day and enjoyed her graduation party.

At the actual graduation, Cleo did not wear a gown, but wore a mortarboard. She wore a black political T-shirt and jeans, and an anti-apartheid white sash across her body. The gown would have cost more, anyway. If Jeni's boyfriend could wear a pirate outfit to graduation, Cleo figured she could be dressed down. Her parents came with Hokusai, or Hoke and her other brother, who she called 'Mad'. The family walked across Foster Hill. Cleo glanced at her old dorm, knowing that, weeks ago, Duane had put his leg through a glass window there. Cleo saw him on crutches. He said that he would never play lacrosse again. Cleo thought of the aging LeBlanc and her memories of the drug taking Uncle Duke Day and Bob playing his guitar on the hill. Cleo thought about The Neville Brothers show, the African and Indian dance performances, and all the concerts she had attended at Middlesex. Mary played Javanese gamelan in a senior concert in the CFA, the shadow puppets moving across the screen like graduates, finally being exposed. The sight of a man wearing a wire, walking across the pristine grass, stopped Cleo's graduation reverie. Cleo knew that 'important' parents were on campus. Then, they crossed the hill, and they saw Bob, sitting there, smiling. Everyone was sedate, as Cleo knew her mom was ill, and looking thin. The family took photos by the Victorian. At least they had this semblance of family. They insisted on it, as if New Haven and Tokyo controlled just one day of their lives.

Cleo's two siblings and her parents rushed to their seats. The same dean who had counseled her in the first year rushed up, asking, "How do you pronounce your name?"

Cleo squirmed. "Lumita Cleopatra Izumi Sugarman," Cleo said, uncomfortably. “Or Cleo or Izzie.” He pronounced the name well as Cleo walked across the stage. William Zinsser gave the graduation speech. He was a friend of Anne Greenbaum’s. Bill Cosby had been last year’s speaker. Cleo knew some secrets about him via some well placed Middlesex students, and she was glad that he was not in town. But, although Zinsser was not a President or a Senator, he was somebody important, and he sent the class off well. The house had to clear out within days, and, ironically, twenty years later, would be named ‘The House of Healthy Lifestyles’.

After leaving Middlesex, the evenings were quieter for Cleo. She worked on her resume, but no one was hiring political activists except Massachusetts Citizens for Clean Energy, so she signed up with the organization. It was evening work. Cleo also worked in late night shifts washing dishes at a diner off of Route Nine. She did not work every day, and some days, she relaxed. She would wake up in the afternoon and go to the Peking Garden All-You-Can Eat Buffet. She then sifted through some of the mementos of her college years and felt the burden slowly erasing itself. One day, after the Chuck Berry concert in the field at UMASS, Bob and Cleo maneuvered the Plymouth through the strip of McDonalds and Kmart that erased the farms from Route Nine in Amherst. Berry, at 60 or so, was running across the stage with his signature leg up, conked hair, and playing his rock ‘n’ roll. The couple decided to go to the Legion for a drink. The usual crowd was there, hollering at Magic Johnson and the Lakers, while some of the regulars played darts. Bob and Cleo looked at each other, laughing about how Chuck Berry must be in his mid-sixties by now, still strutting across the stage. Cleo started to doze on his shoulder, and he smiled.

“There will be no sleeping in this bar,” he said, pushing his long hair back from his tired body.

Cleo smiled and said, "I aint slept in four years."

He chuckled. She felt comfortable in the Legion with Ethel and Bob and Jimmy Brown, sipping her orange juice as the evening wore on. Less stress meant less drinking for Cleo.

"Hey, Maddog's here," Cleo said, laughing gently and pulling the sleeves down on her Middlesex sweatshirt. She looked up to see the tattooed arms on the spindly body of their friend.

"Let her sleep," Maddog said. "She deserves it." He was slurring his words and holding up his cherry brandy. It was always the same, Cleo knew, in this American Legion with its odd light and sound and pulsing of life. Maddog fell slightly, and she turned and held his arm.

"How's the college-educated woman?" he asked. Cleo said that she was fine. She went to the bathroom (they had recently gotten a ladies' room) and, on the way back, Ethel took her aside. She was five feet tall and stout. Her styled hair was graying; her African features were youthful, but troubled that evening.

"Maddog blew a 4.3 on the breathalyzer at the Chuck Berry concert. They kept him in the holding tank briefly and then released him. But he is in no shape to be out. Can you take him up to Greenfield, to the detox?" Cleo knew that he went every few weeks, but there was no ride for him tonight. She walked outside to a sky full of stars and the moon piercing the night and said, "I'll move some stuff in my car and we will go." She went to the Plymouth with its damaged headlights and moved her belongings, her college books and papers and clothes. She returned to the doorway of the bar. Maddog stumbled out with Bob and he laughed.

"I bet you don't know any drunks, do you?" She laughed sadly. "I know a lot, but you are the only one I know that goes to detox…"

He laughed and leaned in, "Got any booze in the car?"

"Just beer, but it's been sitting for weeks," she said. They piled into the car with all of their belongings and Bob carefully slid into the seat beside Cleo, delicately as if he would break something. Cleo turned on the dysfunctional lights and pulled out of the back parking lot and towards the highway. There was something unfathomable about the night, the singularity of the car with all its possessions and her two friends as they barreled down the highway. The Plymouth drove into the increasing darkness and Cleo let the breeze blow through the car, taking with it the Kmart and McDonald's of Route Nine. Maddog slurred, raising his voice, "Where the hell are you taking me?"

"Greenfield," Cleo replied, hitting the gas pedal. The car moved so effortlessly through the trees and over the Greenfield River into Northern Massachusetts. They barreled past towns with the names of Bob's founding fathers, and past the dying mill towns too, towns like the ones Maddog and Cleo were born in. The tires pumped a common liquid rhythm on the pavement.

"You're going the wrong fucking way, you assholes. Pull off the road," Maddog yelled.

"I-91 GOES to Greenfield," Cleo said softly.

He raised his voice again, "It does not fucking go anywhere."

"I wish I had my Dad's special license plate," Bob said. "He was never pulled over."

Maddog stopped for a minute, "Gimmee a beer…Please."

"OK…OK, but you know about open containers," Bob said.

"They know about John Maddigan." Cleo handed Maddog a Milwaukie's Best that had been there since the President's ill-fated cocktail party.

"I'm sorry, I'm sorry," he said. "I'm drunk…you know…I mean I'm…"

"An asshole sometimes," Cleo finished through her teeth, as she listened to him rifling through her college boxes. She thought of what his family and old friends must have gone through.

"We're going to Greenfield," Cleo said. Near Greenfield, the cities were sparse, the lights infrequent, and the Motel 6, Stuckey Stops, and Howard Johnson's disappeared one by one. Only a lonely weigh station was left for Cleo and her passengers. If they went any further, they would have reached the prep school Bob was expelled from, and those camps with the Indian names that the founding fathers stole. She could smell the night air then, coming from up North, coming from the ski chalets and the yacht clubs and the broken glasses of Bob's youth.

"What's this?" Maddog asked, holding something up in a black case.

"My piece of paper…remember?"

"Of course I remember. What's it doing in your garbage can?"

"I'm just packing things," Cleo said.

"It's a nice moon out," Maddog said, changing the subject.

"It looks…turquoise," Cleo said. The orange and white barrels appeared in the night and the dark highway became one lane. Exit 26 for Greenfield became lost in orange flashing barrels that the Plymouth moved through. All of a sudden, the turn off came and Cleo pulled the car off onto the ramp and the rotary and slowly pulled into the town. They pulled towards the quiet Route 2-A. All of its gas stations and motor lodges were closed for the night. She pulled past the stores and the shops and the sleepiness of the Northern Massachusetts night.

"Up the street; it's up the street, take a left," Maddog said.

"It says No Left Turn," Cleo said, slowly.

"Take it anyway," Maddog countered. "I know this town." They took the left turn and proceeded down the residential street. The blue cross shown into the night from the tall and dark building with its ominous windows and shadows. The lonely cars in the parking lot with no passengers made Cleo think about the people in the rooms.

"Just leave me off," he said. Maddog stumbled out of the car towards the buildings and the light of the doorway. He put his hand through the open window and held hers. His veins showed through his wrists and his dragon tattoo stood out, almost illuminating from his arm and across his back. "Thank you, I want to thank you guys for taking me," he said, waving her diploma.

"It's OK, no problem John," Cleo said.

"I really appreciate this," he slurred.

"No sweat, we keep each other going." He stumbled over the grass and urinated on the lawn. Cleo wondered how anyone could blow a 4.3, and smiled a sad smile. Maddog buzzed himself in and they saw a figure at the door.

"It's cool," he called out, "Gotta wait till 12:30."

Sitting on the steps, he was looking at them. An eerie feeling arose and followed them through the silent midnight of Greenfield and back onto the interstate. The papers fluttered in the warm breeze and the trees enveloped the cars once more. Maddog had placed the diploma carefully on the seat, out of the garbage can. Cleo saw the paper in the bluish-green moon: a dragon, whose veins had been pumped out and put back in again, tattooed on a piece of paper.

42

In Amherst, Cleo ran into Mixashawny, a Native American, and an acquaintance of Ed LeBlanc. He was heading to the Rainbow Gathering in the Green Mountains of Vermont. He leaned over from his motorcycle and shouted, "Why don't you two join us." At that time, the people who appeared in the coffee shops, the bars, concerts and gatherings all knew each other. Bob and Cleo loaded their Ames, bought tent into the Plymouth. She drove up the highway and instead of New England slate; there was pot and tofu at the end of their trail. Vermont was like the gates of Heaven, with light from the sun, rolling hills, and the chanting of hymn-like songs. Mixashawny rode by in his motorcycle, his long hair in a braid. Bob and Cleo walked into a circle of people praying. The tie-dye and incense was everywhere, mixing with the low hills and the music. They retreated to their tent, lying next to each other as the Green Mountains spoke their ancient sounds.

As Cleo felt the energy about her, she knew what she had to do. Cleo drove the Plymouth into the quaint New England town. She pulled up by the drug store and walked to the phone booth. She looked at the Norman Rockwell style stores and sighed.

"I'm not coming in tomorrow," she said to the manager of the diner where she worked washing dishes.

"When are you coming in?" the manager said.

"Never," she said, smirking to herself, but feeling her stomach turn. As the hippies in flowing dressed danced to the drumbeats below the sweeping Green Mountains, Cleo saw something on the horizon, in the West.

Cleo and Bob returned to Amherst refreshed. This was a town of 'townies,' but people kept coming in and out of the square, making appearances and then disappearing. Cleo knew that if she stayed, she too would become one of the local crazy characters, someone who could not be taken seriously. In downtown Amherst, both Jeanne and Cleo ran into Mohammed, the dreadlocked son of the Tanzanian revolutionary who was friends with Malcolm X. Mohammed washed dishes at the Lord Jeffrey Inn. She saw him at a coffee shop. He said that he was waiting for his Dad. He was always waiting for his Dad to come in from exotic locales to lecture at the local universities. Revolutionary memories were sexy. He explained, "My Dad is staying at the Lord Jeff, and, since I work there, they won't let me in the front. I have to go in the back." Mohammed talked about his plans to go to the London School of Economics. His Dad did not like his dreads.

"That's so ironic, coming from a Revolutionary," Cleo said.

"Welcome to the real world," Mohammed said.

"I'd rather not be welcomed," Cleo said, as Mohammed brushed his hands on his dishwashing apron. Mohammed told Jeanne that he was planning to do a documentary on the Angolan Civil War. Suddenly, he disappeared from his daily seat at the coffee shop. Jeanne heard that he was accepted at the London School for Economics. He had options. Cleo did not. She knew that she needed friends. She called Niema.

At the Wheel House, the local dive, the bartender looked at Niema and said, "I can refuse service to anyone." Cleo remembered Mohammed going into the back of the Lord Jeff, and things added up. In the morning, she picked up the payphone outside of the coffee shop.

"I have been sending out resumes from my post office box at the new 'Mailboxes, Etc.', and nothing is coming back, Bob, Dan has offered me a job in Eugene," Cleo flatly said to Bob. They were having a beer at the Legion.

"Oh," exclaimed Bob. "That's interesting."

Cleo was in the class of 1988. Wall Street was humming, but the proceeds had not come to her. Bob knew that he was drinking too much rum at the Legion as well. It was still summer, and the festivals were in full swing in Oregon. Bob and Cleo talked for a week about the options.

"There is work for you as well, working to shut down Trojan Nuclear Power Plant," Cleo said as they ate dinner at an Indian restaurant.

"Well, the beer is better, "Bob replied.

"OK, let's prepare," Cleo said. "We don't have much to pack." Cleo paid Billy Scott a six-pack to wire up the exhaust on the Plymouth, which was falling off. In front of Jeanne's apartment, Billy wired up the metal, sending Cleo off with a heft of his Rolling Rock.

43

Cleo drove the 'full to the brim' Plymouth to North Mills. She pulled into the rock house. The drive seemed so fast compared to when her brother had dropped her off four years before. The stone arch above the driveway was sagging. A couple of pigeons sat beside the driveway. But Cleo's Dad was not the stereotypical boxer with his pigeon coops. He was seventy-one years old and his body was sagging too.

"I'm going back to Oregon," Cleo said over sushi rolls.

"I thought you were going to live in Amherst, closer, Lumita-chan," her mother said.

"I have a job running a political office," Cleo said.

"That school was worth it," her Dad mumbled. Cleo knew he had not paid a dime, but stayed silent.

Cleo scratched the rash on her inner thighs, which came from the heater on her Plymouth, which was always on. She could hang around the Legion and talk about Camus, but fixing her car was another matter. Her Mom shook her head and whispered to Hokusai, or Hoke, who was home from an engineering job. Hoke looked disgusted, as if Cleo were a toddler who had broken a toy. He grabbed the graduation gift toolset. Climbing into the hood, like a mad scientist, he clamped up the heater hoses so that they would not spew heat into her car. The job looked as 'Rube Goldberg' as their house. He looked like a forty year old man, with muscles bulging under a generic blue T-shirt. He showed Cleo how the clamps and little pieces of wood shut off the flow of heat.

"Thank you," Cleo said.

"Just don't crash again," Hoke said, mumbling. Later, the mechanic in Oregon said that this procedure was very dangerous, and might have wrecked the whole car. But, like the Izumi family watching her mother leave on the HinanoMaru, the Sugarmans stood outside their old house and waved goodbye. Cleo's mother looked fine, and so the thought of her cancer and Cleo's leaving did not worry Cleo too much.

Cleo drove quickly through the town, through the roads she knew like a child's first book, read over and over. She quickly exited past the airport and onto I-91. She drove the route that she took on her middle school trip to Washington DC, where the teacher who escorted them had flirted with her. She wondered where he was for a second, but then saw the sign for the George Washington Bridge and had to concentrate. She paid the toll and entered New Jersey. On the turnpike, in eight lanes of traffic, she heard a sound. It was quick and loud, like the sound of the assailant's car that comes to a stop in the cop shows. She instantly pulled the car, with its flapping tire, to the side of the road. She shut the engine off in a safety 'pull out' zone. The cars were whizzing by like missed opportunities. Cleo had everything piled in her trunk. She thought that, if the Plymouth was hit from behind, it might all go up in flames.

A brown truck pulled over. A fit man with a little stubble on his face got out. He was a middle-class man, about thirty, the kind Bob was the opposite of – good with a wrench, a steady paycheck, and a tiny home in a far-flung suburb. He rapidly got to work, but they had to take everything out of the trunk. Cleo quickly pulled out books, her high school yearbook, winter clothes, photos, college notes, and journals and threw them on the ground. The man got out the jack and the tire iron and jacked up the Plymouth and put on the tire, a snow tire. This left her with an unbalanced car, as if it had a life in two seasons – one snow tire and three regular tires. She quickly threw everything back in the car, as people were honking horns and making noises. Cleo felt their movement. The man efficiently waved goodbye and Cleo thanked him.

Bob could tell her about the Situationist International Anthology, but could not quickly change a tire. She felt a twinge of guilt then, about the uprooting. She pulled her car back out onto the interstate. I-95 bisected the East Coast corridor like a ready to collapse artery. As she accelerated, she realized that she had no real career connections on this Interstate Eastern artery with its major city/organs pulsing with other people's 1980's lives. That afternoon, she also realized that she had lost her journal about her time in San Francisco with Bob.

The Plymouth roared on into Southern New Jersey and Delaware and Maryland. It was getting dark when she hit DC. It was easy to get into the District. She pulled down into the city, right near Lafayette Park and Pennsylvania Avenue. She parked and walked up to The Vigil. Bobby Lee was sitting there, along with Charles, Ellen and Thomas, and Concepcion and her signs.

"Hey, Bobby, I came to say bye, I am going to work for a peace organization in Oregon," Cleo said.

"Well, it's not the real struggle, like here, but good luck," Bobby said. She talked to Bobby for a while, and noticed that his eyes looked 'out there'. "You know me more than almost anyone," he said, as they hugged and said goodbye.

As the sun set on the White House, Lumita Cleopatra Izumi Sugarman left the East Coast. She drove and drove on the freeway through Maryland, hitting Pennsylvania. She was exhausted, but there were no rest stops on what was now a lonely highway. Cleo had never checked into a non-Tenderloin hotel by herself, and had only a certain amount of money for the trip. They needed Bob's money to rent a place in Oregon. She rolled off the highway, into a small, quiet town with a blinking stoplight, like the one Peter owned. Cleo pulled in the back of some closed down stores, her eyes closing. She lay back in the front seat, drifting off to dreams about Middlesex without any troubles. She jolted at the sound of a bullhorn. She looked up and saw the blue and red lights and wondered if she had paid her insurance that month.

"What are you doing?" the officer asked, as he stared into the vehicle full of books and clothes. "You can't do that, you need to follow me," the officer said. His cruiser, the boxy style 1970s American made cop car, began to turn through the town, in what seemed like a maze. Cleo saw a small town square and a park, as well as a police department complete with a blue light on a pole. She noticed a car with an old red light on its roof. She followed the officer, and she saw that they were headed for a secluded area. In one of her first, real, adult moments, Cleo saw the small sign for the highway, and she pushed it to the floor, taking the ramp and rushing fast onto the westbound lane. Cleo merged into traffic. She placed her car between two semis and kept on going. At least she could now explain herself to a State Trooper, who would know what the town cops were up to. Cleo had been driving for twenty hours when she finally found a rest stop.

She rubbed her pus-filled eyes and felt the summer heat, the buzzing of insects and the smell of garbage. She looked up and saw the entrance to the rest area with its concessions and bathrooms. Cleo unwound herself and went up the stairs, stretching her legs. She walked past the boxes with hotel coupons and tourist brochures, past the area maps and advertisements. She walked towards the bathroom. At the McDonalds, she blinked her eyes. Cleo saw men and women in the line that looked as if they had popped out from her high school history book. The women wore white caps, with their hair pinned; the men had mutton chop whiskers and black top hats. They were ordering their Happy Meals and McDlts. Cleo had to pack her own food, and she felt hungry. 'Even the Mennonites had a better sense of family than me,' Cleo mused. She saw, from her tourist gaze, that they had an insider status, community, and that they knew where they lived.

Cleo barreled on and on, through Ohio. On the outskirts of Gary, Indiana, on I-80, she saw the belching of industrial America, in its last gasps as her mother's country was emerging to compete with it. The interstate was changed with the rapid movement of products and people. She slept at the rest stops, washing up at the bathrooms. She pulled into Chicago, where she drove to Ed Boykin's apartment. He was studying for a PhD in Medieval Studies at the University of Chicago. Cleo watched the elevated train go over them, carrying their youth and optimism with it. Ed and Cleo went out to a diner and talked about Middlesex, which seemed like the distant train tracks heading out of town. She left Chicago and went out into the vast Midwest and prairie. She traveled across the farm country, admiring the long stretch of horizon, the ochre of the sunsets and the wise sky above her. Interstate 80 through Iowa and Nebraska reminded her that she was lucky that North Mills had at least been close enough to libraries, bookstores, and oceans. She slept in the big car, but always kept a wrench in her hand in case of any problems. It was a revelation seeing Wyoming, spread out with cattle, windmills and horses. Unlike North Mills, these ranches and farms were not for show.

Cleo stopped to call Dan, Bob, and others at a lonely payphone. She was tired and went off into the night. The rhythm of the road and diner coffee kept her going for another six hours. She realized that she wanted to look up a number. She searched in her purse for her address book. Cleo saw it in her mind, sitting there on top of a pay phone in rural Wyoming. She quickly pulled into another diner, grabbed another cup of coffee and headed back east on the highway, driving for another six hours. That book held all she had in life: her friends, contacts, and postal addresses. When she arrived back at the booth, she noticed that no wind had disturbed the lonely, small mini-building with its wired connections to the world. She grasped the book in her hand – Mary was in there with Jeanne, Jeff, Peter, Henry, Ed, the Educational Council, the LeBlancs, Mary and Moonstone, the Palming Street people, Oregon Share people, and the Greenworks people. Her family contacts were written in faded letters next to the names of high school friends, tobacco friends, and others from her more distant past. As the sun rose, Cleo cradled the book, looked back at the highway stretching east, thought about the reason she still had snow tires on her car, and turned the Plymouth towards the West. As she drove, she assumed that this prairie that she was in, was a literary and cultural wasteland, except for the Natives. She saw somehow, that these areas held a great literature of their own, with a wonderful plainsong that rang just as loud and literate as New York.

Cleo merged onto I-15, which took her to Utah. As she entered the Salt Lake area, she saw the Great Salt Lake, its crystals washed up on the side, waves lapping, and fossils of ancient life in a desert land. The spires of the Mormon temple peaked up. Others had been forced West, but with different and more pressing reasons. It was difficult to find her old boss Mary's house. The streets all emanated from the giant temple, with directions like 'East South'. Mary Oakton had returned to the site of her earlier life. Last year, she bought a small house in a nondescript neighborhood. Cleo pulled up to the bungalow, thinking about the contrast between Berkeley and Mary's new neighborhood. Mary somehow had procured her usual box wine in a nearly dry state, and giggled and talked politics with Cleo, her cheeks turning red. She was just elected as an alternate to the Democratic Convention from Utah. She was soon to see the team of Michael Dukakis and Lloyd Bentzen at the Omni Hotel in Atlanta. She was excited to hear her hero, Ann Richards, speak along with Jim Hightower, Ted Kennedy, and Lloyd Bentzen. Cleo told Mary that she was going to an office where even the Democrats were the enemy.

Cleo turned the Plymouth towards the North. She crossed Idaho on I-84 into Eastern Oregon. She took Highway 20 from Burns. The names of the small towns began to emerge, where Peace organizations had only one or two members. Mostly, people in these areas were not interested in recycling and saving the world from nuclear disaster. Later, talented and committed writers and environmentalists would live in the same towns Cleo was crossing in her gas guzzler. Then, as she saw the pines emerge near Bend, she began to feel as if she had a purpose. She began to believe that the movement had not ended, and that, over those mountains, the last vestiges of the dream existed. She saw the sign for The Livestock Auction and drove on. After gassing up, she took the Plymouth, with its one snow tread, up the Santiam Pass on Highway 20. The road wound around and the volcanic rocks spoke of tens of thousands of years of physical history. Three Fingered Jack stood to the North, and Mt. Washington to the South, cascading their snow-capped faces at her like the Himalayas. The cinder cones and tuyas of the land would be there even long after Cleo. She saw a small lookout over the vast expanse of mountains.

This Lookout had a wide view of the Pacific Northwest. It was the part of the west so vast, and she knew that they could not fill all of it with the trendy boutiques of San Francisco. There were still places for hippies to hide. That lookout tower made of rock was perched above, as if there had once been a small castle, a bastion against the hordes of invaders from the East. Cleo saw the bristlecone pines and wide vistas. The huge Plymouth came down the mountain. She was an amateur driver trying to make sure that she did not pitch into the volcanic beds below. Detroit had made good cars for the long haul, however, and Cleo was OK. Highway 126 led her into a familiar territory. The lodge pole and white pines turned to the bushier Ponderosa pines of western Oregon, and the rivers ran cool, clear, and bubbling with pristine water. The Willamette Valley approached, with the Douglas fir, the state tree of Oregon, appearing by the roadside. She drove past the turn off for the Cougar Hot Springs. The small cabins and the hippie vehicles began to emerge. Cleo heaved a sigh of relief and kept going, past Springfield and on into Eugene. As she drove on Coburg Road, over the bridge, she saw the old grain elevator and train depot emerge and she pulled down into town. She drove past the Oregon Electric Station restaurant, with its brick, wood and brass, and into the Growing Market parking lot, with its murals and battered exterior. Cleo went through the heavy metal door and up the stairs where Dan Johnson, Gary Kitchens, and David Zuman greeted her, amidst the petitions, protest signs, clipboards, and radical magazines.

Cleo worked that day, helping to organize the canvass. After work, she walked down the stairs past the dreadlocked 'Earth First' activists to the Plymouth. She got into the car, and it did not start. She had driven 3000 miles and the car had quit, as if saying, 'Enough'. Of course, hippie help was readily available. A man in overalls patched it up and Cleo drove up to the communal Hawk House, on Hawk Lane, on a hill on the outskirts of the city. She drove onto the property, which was shaded by trees, with a large dirt and grass driveway in front. Cleo and Bob would be living at the house with Dan and many others. The rent was $82.50 a month, but the room was available only for two months. Ruby Begonia, of 'Get Fried Rice', lived there, and, luckily, he was also a mechanic. He easily fixed the Plymouth for a minimal fee. The Hawk House had a sauna made of local wood, a fire pit, an organic garden that Dan tended, and a small forest of Old Growth trees in the back. Dan's dog, Rosie, ran around the property. Ruby also brewed his own 'Ruby brew' root beer and beer. There was fresh brew, fresh vegetables, and Old Growth trees. Bob would be in heaven. And he was.

44

When Bob arrived at the train depot right next to the office, parties were in full swing. The summer festivals of Oregon happened every weekend. Cleo and Bob were given clipboards and sent out to the festivals to gather signatures for various initiatives, like shutting down the Trojan Nuclear Power Plant and saving the Old Growth trees. They were paid 5 cents per signature, and, with ten petitions on your clipboard, it could be a decent day's work. But, of course, one had to stop and listen to the music and have a micro brew. Cleo also continued her job running the Peacemakers 'foot canvass' with Dan, going all over the Willamette Valley with him, collecting money for peace and justice. One day, a conservative Republican in the Bethel/ Danebo area threatened Dan. The man's American flag was flying proudly. "Hey, I served the country and the flag," Dan said. He high tailed it out of there when the man told him that he had a gun. Cleo began to phase into the phone canvass, having people pick up the checks at the member's homes. Two weeks later, a skinny man with a bandana showed up in the office. He was Jay Macantee, from Missoula. He had a puppy that was named Freedom. Freedom followed him everywhere and was a staple on the office couch. Jay was also 'slinging' and used that money to eat and drink at the Oregon Electric Station next door. The party was on.

After the two months, the kind people at the Hawk House said that Cleo and Bob could stay as long as they wanted until they found a place. They would, however, have to sleep in sleeping bags in the woods in the back of the house. A stray Beagle mix named Snowy came by and snuggled with them in their bags. She waited for them when they got back from the office and from town, wagging her tail and licking their faces. Bob smiled across his bearded face in a way that Cleo had never seen before. He petted Snowy and looked over to Cleo as the sun fell beneath the Old Growth trees.

Bob decided that they would spend every weekend exploring the woods, lakes, rivers, streams, and the coast of Oregon. They went everywhere from camping in Sisters, to Sahalie Falls, to a Peace Festival at Odell Lake in the mountains, and many other locations. They took the dog that Bob renamed Maya, after the ancient culture. She jumped from the back seat to the front seat, laying in their laps and licking their faces.

Cleo and Bob went to the office one day and came back to the Hawk House that afternoon. Maya did not greet them. A group of hippies were playing drums in the main room. "You never said you were officially adopting the dog," they chimed. They had taken her down to the U of O, placed a sign on her neck, 'I'm Snowy, and I need a home.' Cleo and Bob got in the car, rushing to the tree that Maya had been tied to. They asked the pedestrians if they had seen the dog. People said that they had seen her. Bob and Cleo searched the area for hours to no avail. They went back to the Hawk House. Their baby had been snatched. They lay down in their sleeping bags, holding onto each other. They awoke to the licking of their faces. Maya/Snowy had walked the ten or so miles back by herself. All three of them hugged each other.

Maya was there when Chris Martin visited. Chris was a friend of Cleo's from North Mills. He played guitar and had enjoyed talking politics with Cleo. He came when the hippie wedding of a couple, Joe and Cathy, was to take place at the Hawk House. Cleo noticed the trust cheques for Joe coming from a New Jersey address. Chris pulled up in his old Toyota Land Cruiser. He was greeted with all the stereotypical elements of hippie life: the old time string band, the microbrew, the pot and the organic feast. He got out, sporting a peace sign necklace and a fringe jacket. They hugged.

"C'mon, see where I work," Cleo said. He followed her to the Peacemakers office, where more tripsters were in full effect. The Martins and Chris had let her go a long time ago, and now he was giving a last chance at reaching out. They had visited her at Wesleyan, but did not want to see her dorm room. They wanted to go home.

"Tell the people in North Mills about this life," Cleo said, as Chris climbed into his Land Cruiser.

"I will," he said. "It looks like you are having a lot of fun." She watched his vehicle leave, like a postal truck going back to its empty warehouse. Finally, Bob and Cleo found a rental on Polk Street, not too far from the river. The landlady nervously got out of her car, a gently used Subaru.

"Hi, my name is Shirley," she said. She had dyed hair and was smoking a long cigarette.

"I'm going through…going through a bitter divorce. I just need to get some money coming in," she said. They shook her hand and gave her a cheque. She handed them a lease, which Cleo signed. The $400 rental cheques were to be made out to a mysterious company, King Investments. Shirley threw her cigarette on the pavement and jumped back into the car, motoring quickly out past the railroad tracks and on to her crises.

98 North Polk Street was a bit broken down, with some holes in the walls, mold (this was, after all, Oregon), and a jerry-rigged stove for heat in our back master bedroom. There was a backyard for the dog, with overgrown blackberry bushes that Bob loved. They knew that they needed to search for roommates. This however, was Oregon, and there were many hucksters and hippie fakers. Cleo was at work

one day when Bob called the office, stating that he needed a decision. There was a trucker at the house who had cash in hand and said that he would be 'gone a lot'. Bob said that he was a bit 'off,' and he wanted Cleo's consultation. Cleo was busy mapping out routes and adding up totals. "Use your judgment," she said. She was tired of taking care of all the official duties. That day, she had also, at the suggestion of a member of the Hawk House, applied at the Natives Program at the 4-J School District.

Cleo walked into the 4-J office and met Twila Souwers, who coordinated the tutoring of the Native American students in the Eugene 4-J school system. The office was right around the corner from her house, but it was a world away. The offices were ordered, the people looked casual/business dressed, and there was no smell of cigarettes. Cleo walked into the office that was decorated with feathers and dream catchers (before they were fashionable).

"Wow, you are totally qualified. I finally have a Native tutor!" Twila said, smiling.

"Uh, actually I am Asian American," Cleo said, realizing that this was the first time she had actually said this.

"Well, you look Native," she said.

"I have a spiritual connection to Native culture," Cleo said.

"I am going to assign you to a family called the Birds," she said. "What days would you like to work?"

Cleo scheduled her tutoring for Monday through Thursday, so she could have long weekends. Peacemakers were also very flexible with her. For the first time in her post-adolescent life, she had a decent schedule, which allowed her to sleep eight hours a night. She also did not have extreme pressure and deadlines. With this role, she got to attend Native Pow Wows for the first time, and learn about Native culture. Cleo also had the important responsibility of helping the Native students navigate the school culture, but she had little administrative responsibility.

Cleo entered the home of the Birds. Their mother, Gloria, was busy studying.

"Ché," she called. A young eight year old came out of his room. Cleo stared. He looked like a small version of a Native chief.

"Actually, if you are wondering, he's a direct descendant of Chief Joseph of the Nez Perce," Gloria said. Ché's brother Mayo came into the room. He was bigger and looked Latino.

"It's time for tutoring," Cleo said. "Let's read Chief Seattle's speech." Gloria smiled and Cleo smiled back.

"They don't like me at the school," she said. "They judge me. I am raising two kids and getting my Master's Degree."

"I hear you," Cleo said, "My university years were full of people judging me. I want to make sure these kids have the tools to work in the system."

"Thanks," she said.

"No problem," Cleo said. "Let's begin." At home, the trucker, Tom Kelley, had fully moved in. He informed them, after his second day at Polk Street, that he was a 'Vietnam veteran' who had flashbacks. They found another roommate, Brett, as well. They paid $125 a month a piece. Bob and Cleo each paid $75 a month.

Tom pulled his green colored rig into the driveway. He had the stomach of William 'Refrigerator' Perry and dirty blonde hair that was cropped close to his head. The rig's color was a hybrid of pea soup and apples. Unfortunately, he had to work for logging companies, which was verboten at Peacemakers. He remained out a lot at first, bringing back truck stop girls and items from far afield. He also told tales of his struggle up the Shasta upgrade in the ice and stories of his sleepless nights on the road. He began to grow his hair and go to hippie events.

Tom cooked the truck stop girls steak and eggs with cheap wine and vegetables. When he was home long enough, his eyes would change their gentle blue-green color to the color of a sliced olive, still soupy from the cut. On certain warm days in the neighborhood, it appeared that Haight Street in 1969 had moved with force and intensity to the medium sized town. Dan Johnson called it '100,000 people living in a duplex'. Tom had a tie-dye stretched over his immense belly and he had adopted a little dog. He would walk the dog and tell his stories to people on the street, although he never told them at home. With baggy pants and sagging eyes, outside, as in the park, he was the big, laughing clown speaking on his fictive stage. He said that he had been at protests on the Boston Common. Inside, he was the frown-faced, hallucinatory inverse of that clown, leaving greasy pans in the sink and young girls with scared faces in the bathroom. Cleo knew, at least, that they were over eighteen.

The followers of the Bhagwan Sri Rajneesh lived down the street. They lived near the community garden at its end near the river. The Bhagwan followers still had their orange wardrobe, even after their leader had his compound, Rajneeshpurum, seized after he had been deported from the US for tax evasion and bioterrorism. Cleo wondered how people could follow someone who owned 365 Mercedes (one for each day), and who was addicted to nitrous and Valium. But Cleo was following something, too. The neighborhood was hopping. One day, a photographer from the 'Eugene Register Guard' (people called it the 'Regular Garbage') came by. He was doing a story on 'unique neighborhoods'. Bob, who was watching football, called out 'not to talk to him, because you never know who is an agent.' Cleo directed the photographer to Tree. Tree lived down the street in a step van and was over on Sundays with John, Thom, and others for Sunday football. Cleo labeled the house the HOLHM, or 'House of

Large Hairy Men,' as there were often many there. They lived next to the Wichu Palace that meant, 'What's up which u?' The 'House of the Hairy Mamas' around the corner was also part of the neighborhood. The Hairy Mamas was a band full of hairy single mothers, some on welfare. People shared food and music. No one in the neighborhood ended up talking to the reporter.

It was afternoon and Cleo was brushing her hair, listening to the sound of buzzing flies in the shaded room, ever present with the honey that lay sticky on the counter in the kitchen. The afternoon dripped to evening; the light filtering through the window in strangely shaped spots. Bob did not talk much about the old days anymore, before they had met in San Francisco, but the slow rhythm of her stroking her hair must have set him to thinking.

"It's nice to have a home," he said. "I remember those times being held down by the cops, the life on skid row..." She continued stroking her hair. "I watched the cops fill a syringe with dirty water and they pulled back my arm and laughed," he continued. "I left my WASP connections behind, and I thought I would die on the street or in that tiny apartment alone." Cleo ate her soup out of the pan, watching his rising and falling, listening.

"You wet the toilet paper with the shower," Cleo said, laughing. He said that he did not mean to. "And you know the television is broken," she said.

"You know you don't have to watch television...we have... friends," he replied.

"I have one friend in this town," Cleo continued, referring to Dan. "He's bald, forty-six, and a bit loopy...he smokes a lot of weed... besides..."

"Let's go to the fair," he said.

Cleo bobbed her head and ruffled the fur on Maya. The Ferris wheel was turning above the town at dusk. Bob took her hand and led Cleo through the whirring lights and the food stands, weaving through the high school couples who were whirling around on rides, looking out from their luminescent cages. Cleo saw one of her students there, Katrina, who was the half Black half Cherokee girl. She was standing alone at the cotton candy booth. The tall, heavy girl waved. "Win Katrina something," Cleo said to Bob, who replied that he 'was not much into winning,' but he threw the little balls into the coke bottles ten times; by that time Katrina was gone. With his soft hands, he retrieved for Cleo a many-colored parrot.

"What will we call it?" he asked.

"Puffy," she said.

"Like my eyes when I wake up," he said.

"Kinda," she returned. "Like your fucking liver..." He sighed. After the carnival, they put Puffy up in the room, on the bookcase, and he watched over the soft slumber, above the moldy socks and the stained rug. Bob lay on the Mexican blanket with his arms around Maya, who, after her spaying at the vet, had used the moment to make the bed hers as well. Cleo watched them, smiling, and gathered twenty-four cans of Miller to return for coins for the laundry. The laundry sat across from the home brew store and the Dari Mart. Last week, all of her T-shirts, the fabric paint ones from her brother, the Grateful Dead/Bob Dylan shirt, and the Wesleyan shirt had been stolen from the dryers at this laundry.

For the first time in several weeks, Tom had been helpful, and shared the appliances he purchased, including the Braun coffee maker and the crockpot. 'At least he has a job,' Cleo thought. He was always constructing things: a desk for Cleo and other items. He took planks from the loads he was hauling and put together a huge pine bed for Cleo and Bob. He removed the futon, and put it back on top of the bed. The bed just appeared when they were away for the weekend. She told Tom that it was too tall as Cleo was used to Japanese futons that stayed on the floor. He stormed out. "The next time I make a bed, sweetie, I will ask you first," he said as he ground the coffee. She remembered what it was like to not have a home, but like her Plymouth, she hesitated through the languorous summer. She would sit for hours at the desk Tom made; balling up the letters she was writing. People, dating back to Duane, the captain of the Middlesex lacrosse team, seemed to do things for her without asking. Tom complained that she was not good at domestic chores. She pushed away any appearance of middle class suburbia, including cleanliness.

45

It was Cleo's 22nd birthday. The long-haired bus driver took the Green Tortoise bus into the Oregon autumn light, where the leaves of the trees fell onto the streets like foreign bills that were no longer in circulation. The streets were now damp and the leaves were clogging up the gutters. Several weeks ago, the incessant Oregon rain had started. It pattered on the roof and leaked through the bathroom, caving in a part of the wall near the pipes. The hippie festivals ended and people were hunkering down, as if in Alaska, for serious winter drinking and inactivity. Mexico seemed like a good place to go. The Green Tortoise stopped at Cow Creek for a sauna and an organic food meal for the bus riders. Their tag line was 'Arrive Inspired, Not Dog Tired'. After the sun went down, the driver folded down the beds. Cleo found out that fold out beds meant that men could grope women all the way from Southern Oregon and on into California. It was dark and the people pushed up against each other.

Two days later, determined to continue on her sensory journey, she took the shuttle over to Tijuana. Mexico was a magical, real life, one that had a color like Cleo's, but with music, and dance that were not in her blood. It was not a hippie Grateful Dead dance. She mumbled in Spanish and a taxi driver took her past the garbage dumps and shanties of the poor. She boarded the local bus to Ensenada. This bus had the clichéd chickens, heavy packages, and many Mexican children filling its aisles. Cleo realized that she had crossed two borders in her life and she was never going to be able to stop crossing them. She was like addicts who needed to see new, hazed images from their glazed eyes. In her case, the drug was the road and the world, with all of its spinning, kaleidoscopic imagery that would keep her from facing the day to day.

Cleo returned to Eugene, where the football games were still on and the office was humming with activity. Tom Kelley told her that he had followed the Green Tortoise to California in his truck. Cleo quickly added on some tutoring hours. Ché Bird's school counselor was complaining about "the Indians and why they had to hold onto the past..." The counselor continued on, "I can fight no more forever, wasn't that what Chief Joseph said?" Thinking quickly, Ché and Cleo completed an exhibit on his heritage, complete with a sacred eagle feather and a picture of Chief Joseph. Cleo went to the Pow Wows with Katrina. She watched the Natives spin and dance, feathers, beads and drums filled her sleep. Tom cooked a 'Northwest Thanksgiving', complete with a huge stuffed salmon. He hammed it up with the salmon, and Cleo and Bob followed along.

46

In Oregon, after all the Christmas trees were sold, all the workers had left to other harvests, the rains were steady and rhythmic. When the winter of 1988 set in, the rains stayed that seemed like the end of the earth. People's joints ached, and fevers ran high. The convenience mart lost its sign to the rain. The bare light bulb that shone through the window, served as a beacon for the silence of the pickup trucks with their gun racks, and the grizzled faces that looked out of their wind shields. Injured men in cowboy boots ambled into the neighborhood tavern that was lit up with an OLY beer sign. Unemployed carnival workers shuffled in and out. Livestock grazed on the rocky meadows outside of town. The winding two-lane road with its majestic pines pushing up to the sky carried the logging trucks that Tom drove. Traveling past the virgin water and trees to the large mills near Coos Bay, those trucks were monsters.

On the weekends, the Polk Street house was home for the odd family and their dogs. The weather prohibited the camping Cleo and Bob did to get out of the house. The shack-like room in the back of the house had been a former haven for addicts. The police still drove by, looking for a man named Leroy and his clientele. When it was really damp, people knocked on the door, and Tom, who was normally silent, sent them away with his booming voice. They stoked an old stove in the room, and when it got cold, they threw milk cartons and pizza boxes in the fire and watched them crackle. In his spare time, Tom took small parts from spent machines and meticulously fashioned model airplanes. He sent model trains from the tracks that ran from his room to the stove. Bob drank twelve packs of Miller that finally began to pile up next to the stove. He watched Tom's trains travel swiftly and accurately on the tracks. On Mondays, Tom went down to the Bay Area with a load, leaving lumpy messes in the crockpot. Cleo tried to clean up the messes, but they seemed to add up with his empty Coke bottles that he planned to recycle one day.

As winter set in, Cleo kept working with the Natives in the schools, trying to help them with their struggle to learn modern history and English. Cleo sometimes ran into Katrina in the Safeway after midnight. Embarrassed by the twelve packs in her cart, she would leave them in her cart, and instead would bring Katrina the strawberry Bubblicious bubblegum, her favorite. Cleo wondered what a young kid was doing out so late, but it was not her place, or pay grade, to ask. Cleo went home and wrote her own letters in the frail light, letters that seemed just as hard as those middle school assignments, which Katrina slaved over. One day, Tom came back from a run to L.A. and Tucson. Cleo was on her way out the door when the big green truck came pulling up to the curb, brakes hissing to a stop. He came into the house carrying his cooler and a grocery bag. He said that he had got into some confrontation over his load near the Mexican border and, on the way back, he also had to put those brakes on, going sixty five, on that icy Shasta upgrade. "You know you Indians and Mexicans own this whole damn country," he said, throwing down his cooler. "We stole it from you."

"I am not a Mexican or an Indian," Cleo replied, and she knew damn well he knew what Cleo was; he could see it in her eyes, and he saw the Christmas card from Japan that arrived a while back.

"And why are you so worried about WE and US?" Cleo asked. He told her, "no reason," setting the bag of groceries on the counter. "Look," Cleo said, "I am going to Bi-Mart to buy a picture frame, and Oh yes, I need the U joints fixed on the Plymouth…you promised to do that for me, Bob already reduced the rent for you."

"I don't care if you are Phi Beta Fucking Kappa, letter writer, you gotta wait before I do that job." They laughed together, and he grasped her arm and squeezed it. "Easy on the refried beans," he said. Cleo left for Bi-Mart, picking up some daffodils from the flower shop on the way. Bob had just finished something up downtown, and he returned through the back door of their room. She stepped over the carcasses of several broken machines to get to him. He was wiping his hands and looked up from the telephone.

"He got laid off," Bob said, placing the receiver in its cradle. It was February, and the recycling was getting out of hand, falling out of the cabinets and onto Cleo's head. She told Bob, who was surreptitiously pouring some 'Oregon state liquor store' Bacardi into his coffee, "He's watching cartoons again and what about that damn couch he bought from Goodwill with those loud, red flowers?"

"What do you think? That everyone in this world, this place, has meaningful work? What did you do before you got this job? Didn't he help us with this place, didn't he?" Bob said. They began to avoid the kitchen, eating microwave burritos from the convenience store, or buying a 59-cent corn dog and piling it high with condiments. "You don't leave any pickles for the rest of us," Bob said.

"I know, but its vegetables, I need my vegetables," Cleo said. As the rain dripped through the roof, Bob's hands were full of grass from falling in the backyard. "I'm tired," he said. That morning, they ate a 4 a.m. breakfast of fried chicken from the all night Safeway and huddled together on the bed in a red sleeping bag with water fowl scenes flying across the fabric.

"I'm worried about Tom," Bob said. "I think he's losing it since they laid him off." Cleo replied that it was likely because of his 'young passengers'. Bob said that that was ridiculous and that the company was losing money. "We must give him love," Bob said. Cleo agreed, rolling her eyes. "You know you should stop eating that junk from the convenience store," Bob said. "You're getting sick. I don't want that." The light was playing in his eyes. Cleo knew that Bob had been throwing up blood; she saw the spots in the doorway, and saw his body hunched over. Cleo was also gaining weight and feeling ill.

"After all," Bob said, "we have got a lot of love to give." He looked at the stuffed parrot and the dog under the low ceiling and the loud flowered couch. The coke bottles and twelve packs were strewn around the house along with Tom's *The Fabulous Furry Freak Brothers* comics and other mounting debris. On Sunday, a guy named CAT Diesel Power came by. He wore his CAT Diesel Power hat. He asked about Cleo's car, asked about her, but Tom sent him away, saying that he could fix all of the cars on the street. But Tom did not do anything to the man. He slept until 11 a.m., stealing glances at Bob and Cleo. The three of them did not talk much, and Brett was rarely home. But then, Bob used Cleo's favorite dress to wipe his hands. He didn't mean to, but something set her off. "You drunk," she screamed the kind of scream that was a 22-year scream, "Goddamn you." She leaned against the counter, and a Henry Weinhard's bottle broke and shattered. The sound could be heard in all of the converted school buses down the street. Bob took Maya for a walk up to the butte in the moonlight, packing beer cans into his rucksack. As he returned, Tom saw him come through the door. Tom took all of the dirty pots and pans from dinner and threw them one by one into the plastic garbage can that was indelibly speckled with food stains.

"Brother," Tom said, "I'm moving next door." Bob turned away, removing a toy train track.

Bob then turned around and said, "Let's be gentle with him." Cleo said that it was too musty in the trailer and that Tom 'would be back.'

Indeed, he was back; unpacking all of his cardboard boxes. There was a bandage on his hand.

"Cut myself making planes. Looks like I will have to go to the clinic," he said. "Might be infected." He continued, "this guy Francisco came by, looking for you guys, I sent him away, looked like he was jonesing..." Cleo opened up her mouth to speak, but Bob's hand rose up to cover her mouth. She stopped. That night, they all settled in after a late movie. Cleo woke up sweating in the sleeping bag, comforted only by the barriers of the railroad tracks and the river on each side and the tacked up rugs and the daffodils in the wine bottles. She stayed up until the feeling subsided into the colors of the morning streaming into the window.

47

February slowly turned itself into spring. President's Day went by as the Native kids struggled with school. One evening, Cleo brought Katrina to a Powwow. Katrina's black father was unsure about whether to let his daughter go, but he entrusted the child to Cleo's care. Cleo drove Katrina up the neon strip of Highway 99, past the truck stops, RV dealerships, gas stations, and basketball games of Friday night. When she arrived, she was startled by the flags of two nations held by the Pow Wow officiant – the stars and stripes and the feathered flag. Katrina danced in a circle with other Native children and their mothers and fathers. Cleo saw the families who emerged from the homes and the streets and the schools. "On our grandfather's earth, the elk ran wild and the fish swam in the streams," the old Native man said. "These clothes all mean something, the bells on my feet are churches." The drumming in Cleo's ears made the world spin rapidly; the massacred people of Cleo's dreams, they were dancing.

In the crowd, Cleo saw a junkie couple that she often saw around near the Blair neighborhood. She knew that they could find harmony outside of the Cherrywood apartments in Felony Flats. They stood straight and proud. Pointing to the woman of the couple, Katrina said, "That is my mother." After the dancing, Cleo bought her a 'Native Pride' sticker, which she grasped with honor. Cleo took Katrina home and drove herself to the local Larry and Kathy's 24-hour restaurant. She took out her briefcase, the one her mother had given her, signed some letters, sealed them, and stamped them definitively. That dancing and music was like the dancing Cleo had seen and heard with the LeBlancs. She had been too long away from the world in which there was dancing in her head. She came home at 2 a.m. Bob was looking at her carrying the briefcase. Cleo asked, "Are the highways still on fire?" Cleo went in the bathroom and jiggled the toilet handle that had stopped working as had the hot water. The lamplight showed dimly from the bathroom. Cleo stepped on dog shit coming through the threshold in the back of the house, and she knew it was not Maya's. The door had become unhinged. The bed had no sheet except for a beaten up yellow comforter they had carried around through their travels around the country.

"What are you afraid of, Lumita?" Bob asked, softly.

"The shit, the shit, the dirtiness," she said. "And you know he can hear us." Cleo looked at the beaten blanket attached to the window and the dying plants on the concrete blocks and boards. She glanced over to see a handmade calendar sitting in the corner in the dust. She started to shake. Bob asked her gently if she did not want to sleep with him. The toilet kept flushing. He kissed Cleo's shaking body as the dogs barked outside. His body had not been washed, and his hands were cold, but his sad eyes smiled. He was drunk and could not perform. But it was not for sex that Cleo would stay with him, she knew; it was for those hands that connected the fire highways to the heart. The heart and the hands were the simple and strong reason that she stayed. He looked up after they were done and his head was in those hands.

"I'm trying, I'm trying," he said.

"It's so hard to be this close to you," Cleo replied. He asked Cleo again what she was afraid of. She again replied, "Oh, God, love, the shit, the shit, the dirtiness..."

48

Bob had a meeting of the Marijuana Initiative (MI) in Portland. Paul Stewie, from the New York Greenworks office, was recruiting him. There were several unsuccessful attempts to legalize marijuana in Oregon. It was essentially 'legal' several years before, with minimal fines for possession. But the Feds had cracked down on pot. Bob was known for being a 'people person' and he was bright with writing and speaking in small groups. The word had spread out West. Cleo knew that she would have to be alone with Tom for that time that Bob was away. She watched Bob get on the Greyhound bus, looking like a bird migrating up North. The thought of being with Tom in the house without Bob sent a throbbing, not at the temple, but in the back of the head, which would progressively crawl up the base of Cleo's skull. She came back from work, and Tom was waiting for his unemployment check. He was stumbling from sleep to brew a strong cup of coffee and to begin the endless string of cigarette butts in the small bathroom with the dysfunctional toilet and the warped tiles. The talk was sparse as he ate bowls of Captain Crunch and watched cartoons. He eyed Cleo nervously, and that made her shake.

He had his pot, and Cleo had a bottle of wine from the convenience store. When Cleo emerged from a shower, she saw him searching through her dresser. Cleo turned away and loudly rummaged through the refrigerator, filled with Tom's food stamp food. Amidst talk of spaghetti sauce recipes, they would yell at each other about the transgressions. He did not say much, but, when he did, he made an affair of it. He walked over to the neighbors on Saturday afternoon, telling the Hairy Mama music group his stories. Cleo worked both jobs and hung out with Dan a lot, but it was still not enough time out of the house. Dan and two other guys at the office, Mikel and Bruce, often talked about Dan Millmann's *The Way of the Warrior.* Mikel was into 'rebirthing' therapy, going back to being a baby and coming out clean. Cleo knew that she was left with a baby at home, but he wasn't into therapy. "In Idaho, I still had my pilot's license, until I dive-bombed at those farmers in the potato field…it was a big chase," he laughed. After a while, the fabrications got wild. Cleo felt obligated to visit him in his room, to sit with him through endless cartoons as he meticulously worked on his plane models, telling stories at the rain. There were stories about driving around the country in converted school buses, and being chased over state borders on his motorcycle by at least the whole police force of Alamogordo, New Mexico. That night, it was a full Oregon moon and Tom asked Cleo to visit with him again. His pretzeled fingers rolled a smoke into a fine point. Cleo knew that he had found the tobacco in Bob's drawer. He breathed evenly and slowly. The heat began creeping slowly up her neck. She waited for more fabrications, more stories. After all, this was what he was famous for, and Cleo was beginning to enjoy the stories.

"You know this weather, it's terrible," he said, "I don't know why I moved from Southern California…my back is hurting," he said.

"Yes, well, then you ought to take a bath," Cleo said. The plumbing was working again. She waited for some story about car chases outside of Tuscaloosa, Alabama in the 1970s, or about pig roasts that hosted at least two thousand people.

He looked at Cleo, "No bath. I need the tiger balm…it's just like when I bailed out of the plane…she, the woman, rubbed that tiger balm into my bruise…nothing else would do…wasn't a brand name like now, but the real stuff…" The heat came to Cleo and she began to sweat. Cleo asked Dan to come over, but everyone knew about Tom.

Cleo looked at herself in the mirror that Tom used for the tiniest of planes.

"After that, they wanted me to do another combat mission…I was lying there in the cot all bandaged up and when they came up and asked me to fly one more, I was in fucking bed."

"What did you do?" Cleo timidly asked.

"I got my goddamned gun and pistol whipped the guy…I hated to do it, but I just couldn't take another one."

"Well, you shouldn't have had to," Cleo said. The rain was flooding down. He kept talking. "You know, though, I left both of them behind…" Cleo watched him climb painfully up into the bunk bed that he made for himself, noticing that scratch on his hand still left from the Xacto knife, or perhaps from the bottle Cleo had broken. "Her…and the baby…" He lay down. Dan had a story like that, but there was no baby involved. Cleo felt like checking with the government for the veracity of this story, but she knew that whatever pain he had been through, it was like war.

It was still raining, and Cleo was gaining weight and people were always drinking. Eugene was soggy and she was thinking about her failure at the LSATS. Cleo looked for better, more professional jobs at the U of O career center, but all her letters got no responses. Many required experience with very specific skills or a Master's degree. Cleo thought about getting a degree in counseling, as she tutored and counseled. But Eugene was a small town, and any employer could easily find out about her life. Cleo decided to take the GRE and the Miller Analogies Test. 'But, for what?' she wondered. Cleo called Anne Greenbaum. Cleo had been sending letters, asking for information on different graduate programs. While the guys were watching football and talking politics, Cleo went to Kinkos to type out a long piece of writing. Cleo applied, as Anne Greenbaum counseled, to Master's degree programs at the University of Oregon as well as to places that were 'really off the map.' People who did not want to be part of 'the system' surrounded Cleo. She also had no family help and her mom was ill. Cleo strode into the English Department at the U of O. The secretary told Cleo that the director of the Creative Writing Program 'was absent since 0800 hours.' Cleo knew that she was sunk. The rejections came in, just as the LSAT failure. Cleo was getting used to this. Bob could have been in this world, but he had rejected it long ago. Cleo's drives to the university, failed job applications (even for jobs assisting the handicapped), were adding up. Cleo and Bob were going out less as the money was dwindling, and Tom was getting crazier.

49

The letter came in March of 1989. Cleo was accepted to New Mexico Mining University's MFA program. Bob came home from an MI meeting and Cleo told him the good news. Cleo asked Bob if he was happy for her. "Proud, I am so proud, but you raided the pickles from the condiment bar…look, there aren't any left…you know how Tom feels about this house," Bob said. Outside, the fair was going on again, a carnival. "I know you will make a good college teacher," Bob said. Cleo smiled. She peeked through the door and saw the meticulous precision with which Tom made those model airplanes, glue dripping from his hands.

"You know, my U joints still aren't fixed," she called to Tom.

"Hey, maybe when you get back," Tom said, although he heard the daily clunking of the car. "You are coming back, aren't you? Cleo said yes, but when the program coordinator called on the phone, Tom told her that she wasn't there, that she had moved. A couple of weeks passed, with the usual routine. Before Cleo left for the first time, Bob said, "On the street we saved each other's lives. You saved mine in so many ways. I will never fuck with yours."

"I'll be home soon," Cleo said. "I'll bring wine."

"Top shelf, professor," he said, laughing.

Cleo did not cry when she left from Mahlon Sweet Airport to find her future, but, from the plane, she watched what she thought was the house, dissolving into the hills as if it had never existed. Cleo had never heard of Two Rivers, New Mexico. It sounded exotic. It was almost a PAC-10 school, and the guys watched them play on Saturdays. It seemed to be the last place a 'hippie' student would want to go. Of course, like all of her other odd opportunities and weird timing, it was the only school Cleo got into. And it was only by a lark. Hollywood screenwriter Steve Gellen, who had written the screenplay for a Vonnegut book, fought for Cleo to be accepted into the MFA program. Cleo understood that he wore white suits, smoked cigars, and was involved in an African religion. Single Room Occupancy Hotels, Haight Ashbury bars, and the tobacco fields Cleo worked in, were not too weird for him. Like Cleo's Dad, Gellen's father, a jazz musician, was accused of being a Communist. His family had to flee to Europe, rubbing elbows with Gore Vidal and Dino De Laurentiis. If Gellen knew about her mother's JFK assassination book translations, he would have approved. Cleo stayed with Dan's mother in a suburb of Two Rivers, and she even let her drive her car to NMMU. Her home was in a neutron zone of suburbia, something that Cleo had never imagined with her alternative lifestyle. Two Rivers itself was not what she imagined either. It was a college town, like Eugene, but nothing at all like Eugene. It looked a bit like a mall, with no Natives selling jewelry on the street. Perhaps Cleo wanted to see exotic things in the Southwest. Cleo saw the Circle K Store, the Tune-Up Masters Shops, and the skid row downtown.

When Cleo returned, Bob did not want to discuss the matter. Cleo told him that she would go back and forth to Eugene. Perhaps Cleo should have tried to apply to U of O the next year, but her youth was whittling away like the ends of the rolled Drum tobacco that Bob smoked and she could not wait. NMMU gave Cleo a Regent's Scholarship and a Teaching Assistantship. Cleo called her mother, who was in and out of the hospital, to tell her that she would be teaching at a university. Cleo could not say no.

50

They frequented the convenience store for corn dogs and for more and more twelve packs for Bob. The dinners came less and less often from Tom, and sometimes they were burnt. Cleo wanted to hear about those Idaho State Police officers and their bullhorns, but there were no more stories. Tom, however, stopped her more and more often by the flowered couch and told her what it was like to return. He told her what he had left behind with the part of his body that dropped out of the plane. Cleo listened to him and watched him climb up to his bed, and she let him rest. She highly doubted the fantasy of the pistol-whipping, but she wondered about the rest of it. Cleo called the Hell's Angel, just in case, and he said, "Somebody bothering you?" Cleo replied, "Not really," but kept the number close by as she kept the wrench nearby when she slept. During those times, on the way to schools where the Native kids studied, Cleo turned the Plymouth onto the road near the railroad tracks. She guessed that it was the purples and pinks over those tracks that got in her eyes and caused that intense white light at night. At twenty-two, she could never imagine the ways that the rains could come down in the Pacific Northwest. The brief bright sun and the incessant rain impaired her vision the way that naïve toughness could be sliced thin and liquid on the table in the bare light. Tom was still in the neighborhood, with his gigantic belly roped in, navigating a truck from a temp job into the Roadway Freight warehouse with great precision. "He fixed the U joints," Bob said. "It's your car." She told Bob that Maya was 'his dog', but he said that she was 'our dog'.

"I never told you he put a knife in the cabinet before you left,"

Bob said. "You know, though, he never would have hurt us with that instrument, only himself." Cleo said that she felt that she did not do enough for Tom. "There is no way that we could understand him." Bob replied. "All we could do is love, the shit, the shit, the dirtiness," Cleo said. The beautiful trees peaked up into the clouds as the sun went down, those colors of the Pacific Northwest. The trucks rumbled by and Cleo could hear the ocean hit home against the jagged cliffs north of Florence, where they had taken the Fury one night with the dog and had stood watching the sea, a place to rest. The white light was a sliver between the fingerlike clouds, and the bridge that took the loggers to the mills. Tom began to wear tie-dye and was now working the Saturday Market with the hippies, hauling out the recycling. He no longer visited Southern California, nor talked much about planes. He found a place for himself in that town. Cleo took the Oregon light in, and she knew that she was the one who had infected his hand.

51

Even though Cleo was moving to New Mexico, she was plotting, saving her money to buy her ticket to Europe and a student Eurail pass. Her hallmate at Middlesex, Ed Boykin was studying at the Abbe St. Jean outside of Paris and a friend, Debra (no longer Debbie) was also touring Europe. Debra was moving to California in May and wanted to see what this new European Union was all about. The closest Bob got to Europe those days was the movies that saw at the Bijou Theater in Eugene. Bertrand Tavernier's *Round Midnight* brought the couple to tears. They also went out to the WOW (Workers of the World) Hall a lot, to escape Tom, who had insisted on borrowing $500. His eyes were often bloodshot and his hair was greasy. At the WOW Hall, Cleo and Bob saw John Cipollina, and many other acts from the 1960s. Cipollina still kept his hair cut in the 70's style. The musician, in his old corduroy suit jacket and flare leg jeans, had to be propped up on stage by the mike. Despite Cleo's various range of activities, she sometimes wanted to be like him, propped up. Brett, the photographer, left the house and they rented to Jessi, whose father was an actor on a currently running cop drama. Her grandfather was part of the Rat Pack scene, a man who looked so funny and in control on TV and stage. Jessi said he was a rager, who left a horrible legacy in her family. Jessi arrived to Polk Street, straight from Reno, in an older model red Volkswagen, with a huge Grateful Dead sticker on the back. She, however, still kept miniskirts in her wardrobe as well as *Cosmopolitan* magazines in her closet. She not only came straight from Reno, they later learned, but also straight from a stint in heroin rehab.

Working at John Ascuaga's Nugget in a low-level capacity gave her easy access to the junk. She and Tom got along surprisingly well, getting stoned and listening to Huey Lewis and the News. He was twenty years senior to her, but this friendship did not bother Cleo. She paid the rent. Her drunken and drugged father called the Polk Street house on occasion. Cleo imagined him in his TV cop outfit, chasing suspects.

52

The rain kept coming down, incessant and constant. Cleo purchased her ticket to Europe from an office by the university. When she got home, she noticed that the mold growing in the house was creeping into the kitchen. David from the office began talking about the protests at the Nevada Test Site. Thousands were gathering in Mercury, Nevada to raise their voices against the testing that was going on in this remote area near Native land. Cleo recalled being at Middlesex and reading Joan Didion's essay about this site. In Berkeley, she and Bob had worked for the now 300 plus pound Moonstone, infected as a 'down winder.' Cleo wrote a small grant and David gave her a small stipend to attend the protest.

Eight protestors set out from Oregon in a van. The 'Van Go' headed down through Oregon, the rain splashing against windshield, hippies taking turns driving. The massive mountains of the West dwarfed them, and they felt the hugeness of the country that they were protesting against. The valley spread before them in many colors. It was breathing at them. Cleo wondered why they called it the 'Death Valley'. They all jumped out of the van, speechless. One of the young guys took off his shirt and stood like a Native warrior, peering out onto the vistas. They stood at the edge of the valley and gawked. The West was opening opportunities for Cleo, ones that she could not get to in the enclosed, stratified cities of the East. Here with these people, she felt like part of a tribe. They pulled out of the Valley towards Mercury. This was a desolate land, so far away that the government thought that nobody would come to bear witness.

As they approached the Test Site, Cleo saw the sign for Beatty,

Nevada and also the sign for Scotty's Castle, a castle named for Walter Scott, or Death Valley Scotty. Scotty, she knew, found a place, even in the remotest desert, to stay. He had a purpose, and so did the eight protestors. They pulled in with the other thousands of exhausted people, to set up the tents. They unfurled the antinuclear banner for use in the next day's protest. The desert moon was so clear against a sky full of stars, one that Cleo had never seen. The protestors all snuggled near each other in sleeping bags, and Cleo felt distant from the rain and Tom and his madness.

The next day, one of the leaders in the Shoshone tribe headed the group going out to the site. All the protestors marched in unison, seeing other activists they knew. The famous Greenworks also unfurled a banner, but since they had sprung for expensive rooms in Vegas and had spent some time at the casinos, they were rested. If the members knew about Vegas, Cleo thought, it would surely be a scandal. They all went en masse, chanting and waving banners. Cleo thought of the pictures of the seared Hiroshima victims and was brought to tears. The local police sat in their older cruisers, looking bored. Cleo walked quickly over the line into government property. The officers walked over and, as if in a high school gym class, lined the protesters up. Cleo turned around and felt the plastic cuffs around her wrists. She followed the protestors onto the drab buses. Cleo began to think of all the scruffy activists in and out of the office, many who left children behind, some who had multiple women lovers, and others whose anger was like that of a drill sergeant.

Cleo felt good about what she was doing, but something seemed odd. Cleo felt like she could not do this forever. The Native kids she tutored needed mentors, and she could not be a mentor if she was living in a tent. Cleo would not want Katrina or Ché to live in a tent, even if their ancestors had. The protestors were quickly processed through, and the charges were dropped as there were so many activists there. Again, as at Middlesex, Cleo knew that she had too many contradictions to be an activist. She could not give up driving her car and using electricity. She was an insider in this group, but she could not stay. The next day, they packed up and headed for the long haul back, with the sounds of Native drumming and protest chants in their ears.

53

Cleo had a certain window of magic in her life. She had to go before she became a cautious tourist, viewing the world as a Thomas Kinkade painting, merged and mixed, terribly painted and unintelligible, an adult Eurozone full of Pizza Hut and McDonalds and Sarcozy. She took the Greyhound to Seattle; the huge pen on the side of the building where the bus pulled in blocked her view. She could feel the city's stevedores, captains, and totemic Native animals as she walked down the street, where she met John Gamble, who was having issues at the Greenworks office. He took Cleo to an Asian restaurant in the U district, where he was also working at University Avenue Sports Bar. The long yellow and white buses made creaking noises as they moved up and down the damp streets, their slinky-like grey middles bending. The streets smelled of coffee and fish and Cleo could hear the sound of thrashing music and saw kids walking in lumberjack shirts. They were not hippies.

The music was early Kurt Cobain, who hailed from further out in Washington, the town of Aberdeen, where the logging trucks rumbled into the Olympic National Forest. Nearby, the seals made sounds that could be heard all the way to Orcas and Anacortes. Cobain was on a destruction path, not like the pleasantly stoned hippies at the Oregon Country Fair, or the yuppies who were starting to move to Portland and Seattle, wearing Patagonia and driving SUVs with kayaks on them. Cobain, like Bob, was looking for last chances and places to finish it. He would soon meet Courtney Love, and they would soon be seen struggling, writhing as Bob and Cleo with the pain of the new and the substances that floated about in front of them. John talked about sports, but his eyes seemed brooding and pained. Cleo's tape of Eric Clapton and Derek and the Dominos, *Layla* played over and over as she got on the flight from Seattle to Vancouver. *Why Does Love Got to Be So Sad?* looped over and over. The Vancouver terminal was unnaturally clean, and Cleo felt that this cleanliness was sending her off from the moldy Polk Street House, the huge airliner slinging her across the continent to a different world. The red wine tasted excellent. The food was better than any airplane food Cleo had ever consumed. She watched movies in different languages. She sat back and relaxed in her army pants and political T-shirt.

Cleo landed in Amsterdam, where the Schiphol airport also looked very clean. Debra met her with open arms. She was curly haired, with a head full of numbers and a heart as big as the continent, She had the maps of the city figured out and they went to stay in Vondelpark. As they waited for a trolley, they noticed a man standing there with his little dog. The dogs were everywhere, on the trains, in the cafes, and on the streets. Deb looked at the dog and reached to pet it.

"What is your dog's name?" she asked.

"Adolf," the man replied.

"That's an interesting name," Debra stated. Cleo felt sick. They walked by the workmen dressed in dress shirts and moved on into the city. After parting with Deb, Cleo hit the brown cafes and went to the Marijuana Museum. There, she spoke to people who knew of the 'goings on' in Oregon. She gave the bearded men and hairy-legged women a recent pamphlet from the MI. The museum displayed T-shirts and exhibits from the early years of the movement. Cleo took the train up to The Hague and The Tivoli Gardens. She watched an air show, while lying in the sand on the beach, the first place where she ever saw little striped, tented rooms for beachgoers, as in the old European movies. Cleo then entered the old train heading to Copenhagen, which was on the international hippie circuit. Cleo got off the train and went directly to the intentional hippie community of Christiania. There, Cleo felt welcomed and enjoyed the free hash. She listened to guitar music and toured their gardens, living areas, and communal spaces. This communal life was on a larger scale than the Hawk House or the East Blair Housing Co-op in Eugene. Bicycles flew by and flower scents filled the air. There were places on this planet, Cleo knew, where alternative people could go. But she felt a bit tanned and was tired from the walking. She got on the train to see Ed Boykin. The Eurail was speedy and efficient. He was busy with research at the Abbe. Cleo chatted with Ed, who had grown his hair longer. They went out to eat at a café, which seemed older than the oldest building in Oregon. To say Cleo was amazed with the Abbe was an understatement. Ed, who, at Middlesex, wore lace-up black combat boots and lumberjack shirts, looked just as at home in this location. He was a true scholar, with his round glasses and his command of French.

Cleo went through the streets of Paris with her backpack, going to Musée Rodin, enjoying the gardens, noticing figures emoting in ways she could not get humans to express. She roamed around, purchasing bread and wine. The wine was cheaper than juice. She went to famous graves and monuments. She made someone take a photo of her at the Blaise Pascal monument/gravestone. It was graffitied, like a lot of Paris was at the time. On Bastille Day, Cleo walked down the Champs de Lysees, and would have to report back to Bob, that, yes, there was a McDonalds there. The celebrants helped Cleo to realize that there were other holidays in this world. She began to feel the old streets, the balconies, the patisseries and the boulangeries. She walked the alleys and anticipated going to the museum that she had seen in textbooks. She looked up and her eyesight was jarred with the vision of the gigantic glass pyramids. She had seen I. M. Pei on the cover of those magazines as a youth, and she knew he had talent, but this was a shock. Modernity, postmodernity, and post-post modernity had arrived. Cleo walked among all of the pilfered ancient artifacts, her eyes ablaze with a child's wonder. The statues, the giant oil paintings, the Egyptian artifacts; it swirled around her. She exited the Louvre a new person.

Cleo got on the train headed for Spain. She went through Spain and Germany, viewing the sights. Other young travelers shared their wine and cheese and fruit with her. She walked and took the public transportation everywhere. The languages flowed through her like that wine, with no preservatives or Americanisms. On the German train, Cleo saw what she thought were army officers in uniform. She quickly got on the train and was moving yet again. She partied all night in St. Pauli and was not ready to see the Concentration Camps or to attend classical music concerts yet. The countries and cities moved together like her youth, their names running around her head with an accent. In Brussels, she walked around the Palace and government buildings where she knew that the new European Union was being charted out. She also went to Luxemburg, where she saw the Bock Casements, fortifying the city to keep out smelly people like her.

She traveled on, dazed, drunk and dirty. She was getting weak from the lack of good food and no bed, so she decided to head up to see Kirsten, in Norway. She and Bob had worked with her at CALFORCE in San Francisco. The maze of train schedules and the old time, rolling numbers on the boards in the stations jumbled in her head. The moving of those black schedules with their letters on them, tumbled people from city to city. Cleo got used to times like 0230 and 2015, rapidly changing currencies and getting her passport stamped.

The document was filling up, like her, with color and patterns and experience. She kept it close to her body and saved the loose change-francs, Deutschmarks, gilders. All the shapes, sizes, colors and patterns were dazzling, each with their different queens, kings, flowers and flags. Cleo tried to think of Eugene and the Tiny Tavern and blues at the Butte and Sunday football, but she wasn't there; she was on that different continent with her big bag and expanding mind. The train up North took longer. The men had Carlsberg beers in hand at 8 a.m. It was odd to think it was hours earlier in Eugene, people sleeping, even at Middlesex and in New York. As the train pulled into Basel, she saw the Swiss flag, as she had seen in the Olympics and on movies with ski scenes. Next, she got out and roamed around Sweden. Its small shops and clock towers and trees reminded her of parts of New England. The train moved on and soon it was night again and they were moving over water. She felt the dark ocean beneath her, darker and deeper than the Atlantic. She had passed those farms in her Fury, driving west, and now she was connecting generations and continents in her young mind. She knew that deep, deep fjords were near here and she could feel the ice, the trees, and the lonely sounds of cows and livestock.

"Lumita, Lumita," a jet-black haired woman called towards her. Cleo stared. She waved and Cleo came to her, hauling her big backpack. All of the small cars were opening and closing their doors. They walked down to Kirsten's car…it was a huge, American car. Kirsten had had to go home from San Francisco as her visa had expired and there were issues to deal with. Cleo knew there had been great tragedy and the cold winters and the bad business that her family had was not at all fun for her. CALFORCE had been a refuge for her too. Kirsten and Cleo went out in the big car and people were staring at the two black haired women. Kirsten gassed up, saying that the petrol was very expensive. They headed for Svartskog, where Kirsten lived, talking the whole way. She was not happy in Norway, but there were no other alternatives. It was like Cleo's North Mills to her. Cleo went to Kirsten's home, however, and her mother had cooked an amazing meal for Cleo, the first real meal that she had had in two weeks. She ate with gusto and fell into the bed, glad to have a bed and a shower. Kirsten and Cleo toured the town and city, going out for a glass of wine and coffee. Cleo told her that she hoped she could make it to the US, but could not imagine her at Polk Street. She realized how different the alternative culture was in the US. There were shady elements, drugs, so many odd things that she knew existed in Europe, but she realized that American counterculture had freedom and its nationwide network was available, but, unlike Europe, the social service network was not always available to catch those who fell through.

Morocco seemed to call Cleo. The LeBlanc family had been there in the 1970s with Randy Weston. The drumming sounded in her ears. Cleo had read her father's autobiography carefully, and she noted the part about 'Portuguese in Bermuda' which meant that they came from the Azores, not too far from Morocco. She felt the primordial push. The train moved down into the belly of Europe. Cleo decided to go to Italy first. The air was electric and the red wine flowed through her like a new, transplanted organ. The vines and fields and towns sang to her, the perfumed kerchiefs and dough and spices mingled. She got out in Rome, and the city whirled about her like Antonini and Fellini and Marlon Brando were here all at once, embracing her. The smog and little cars and scooters ran about. Cleo felt her womb and breasts and eyes and nose move her around the city. Cleo walked and walked, with no money for taxi, watching the buses go by that she could not figure out. She walked all the way to the Coliseum, which stuck out like an ancient reminder that games will always be with people, no matter where they go.

A young man picked up Cleo and drove her around Italy in a scooter. Cleo went to the Vatican, and the Sistine Chapel, looking up at the ceiling. She thought of all the wars waged for religion, all of the women oppressed, as Cleo had learned at Middlesex. But she knew there was beauty in this devoutness, in people's fervent need for ritual. She had seen it in the Natives, and it was older. Cleo wandered and wondered; her feet got dirty and body got exhausted. The train to Brindisi was full. They were at the peak of their youth. The wine bottle was opened, the singing began, and all of them forgot about class differences, parentage, and language. They put their arms around each other as one nation and the ride went on. In Brindisi, they exited for the ferry to Greece, which was no cruise line. Cleo changed currency yet again, getting some Drachmas, the huge coins feeling like they were from the ancient times. She put them in her bag and rushed to the ship. She would be traveling third class, which meant that she would be traveling on the top of the ferry, through the night. They inspected her pass. She climbed to the top, and she heard the blowing of the horn, the beautiful sound of passage. It was a gorgeous day across the Adriatic Sea. There were few clouds and the sun was out. Cleo stretched out in one of the large deck chairs and wrote in her journal. Cleo also read a *The Nation* magazine that Ed had given her. She read that Americans were sick of Reagan, but Dukakis was not much of an opponent to the Republicans. They were still in funny business in Central America, and nothing much had changed. Her Middlesex roommate Sarah's revolution had not come, despite the new Earth First activists that were beginning to pop up in Eugene, and, of course, Bobby at the vigil in front of the White House. Cleo also read French poetry and the Beats, her head full of radical and useless ideas. She was never going to get tied down to Bethel/ Danebo, North Mills, or any other ridiculous suburban, middle class idea. She was on a boat, and on the top deck and heading for points south. It began to get cold.

Cleo had been partying with some couples from the US and Italy and Spain, and they drank and ate bread and salted fish. The sun was up and the sky clear. The setting of the sun over the Adriatic was ancient and mythical, with satyrs and pots of mead and stringed instruments. Cleo settled into the deck chair with her jean jacket. The wind began to get stronger as the ferry chugged through rough seas. Cleo's body shivered to its core, but she had nowhere else to go, and so she had to go into the unknown, like NMMU, the middle of nowhere, bare to the elements. Cleo shook all night, her toes freezing and her body aching. Finally, the sun peaked up and they began to see land. The sea was not as choppy and the sun was beginning to emerge. In Athens, Cleo walked miles and miles once again, up to the Acropolis and the Parthenon, looking at Athens and the ancient/modern world about her.

From Greece, Cleo headed back to Italy and then to Southern Spain, where she would catch the boat to Morocco from Algeciras. The port was teaming with products and people. Cleo knew now that some of her ancestors must have been in these areas. At the ticket office, she got a round trip ticket to Tanger, discounted with her Eurail Pass. The queuing to the boat was confusing, with a lot of jostling. Cleo met a man, Chuck, from North Carolina. As the boat pulled out, Cleo panicked a bit, knowing that she was going to another continent. But Europe was disappearing and the Rock of Gibraltar was appearing. Her head buzzed with jazz and secrets. The sea was so blue, with no clouds and Cleo saw people with hooded garments and scarves. She listened to a musical language that flowed from their lips. The passengers alighted and went down the plank. They walked to Tanger, to the Square where snake charmers and fishmongers and men with trained monkeys and turbans walked out of a movie. Like roadside Native American hawkers, they motioned to Cleo and Chuck. Hawkers sold clothes and spices and wares. Cleo felt at home. The Moorish architecture and alleyways to secret senses appeared. Now, it's a complete tourist spot, but then it had mystery and danger. Berbers were selling goods and Cleo looked like them. They drank the green, sugary mint tea and walked and walked to the train station, going by men smoking hookahs and talking in large groups. They bought the tickets to Marrakech, and Cleo let the name slide off her tongue, Marrakech.

The train was another thing, not like the European trains... ancient and with a sound that was like the movement of industrial devices from the 1800s. They pulled out and the colors moved before Cleo. The train pulled out of the city, with families and animals and smells of batbout and mutton and the sound of ancient music. The train lurched. Cleo looked out the window to see desert and palms. As they went further, Cleo strained to see the Atlas in the distance, where Berbers moved and sang and traded. The sun went down as an old man came through the car, ladling soup out of bowls for a few coins. They bought soup and bread. The old man's hood moved and Cleo saw his veins in his neck and his eyes, dark like hers. Chuck talked a bit, but Cleo was in her own world. They slept as the train moved into the night. Finally, they arrived in Marrakech, and Cleo could tell that they were no longer at a port. Africa was coming up from its belly, with traders and hawkers and turbans and robes of all kinds.

Cleo wondered what it must be like in the Sahara below and further down in the regions where slaves had been sent to America. Ancestors of some of these people must have done that trading and moving of people. Oppressions were everywhere, no matter the beauty. Women were segregated, moving in their own groups. They moved through the square bartering and buying food. The alleys were winding and it seemed impossible. They got lost and wondered if they were tricked. Around every corner was a dead end, a maze. All that Cleo had left at home was the $60 she had left with John Gamble, making him promise not to spend it. Here she was in Morocco, and John was struggling away at the bar and the office. Bob was home, playing music and reading political magazines.

The train went on and some guys sat next to them in the creaky wooden seats. They were 'guides' out of some bad Hollywood 'adventure gone wrong movie'. Cleo thought that they would take them to an alley and grab everything. They smooth talked Chuck. Cleo had to follow. They told them of a seacoast city, Asilah, that they must go to. Chuck took the bait. They got off the train and got on another one to Asilah. As they approached the city, Cleo realized that the guides were not lying. It was indeed beautiful. The seaside breeze was warm as they had tea with these men. They were bargaining with Chuck over some small rugs. Cleo listened and smiled as they told her she looked like a Berber woman. Cleo had an Indian print dress that was basically made out of an Indian print bed throw that had been altered.

"You also look like those hippies that came here in the 60s for hash," they said. "Do you want hash?"

"Oh, no, of course not," Cleo said, having heard of *Midnight Express,* knowing she could not get into anything. Cleo said that she was just waiting, and would buy later. Chuck did enough buying for her. She brought a tiny token hookah and was done. Chuck was asking about apartment rents, and Cleo tugged his arm, insisting that they had to go catch the train. They ran, quickly saying bye to their guides

One of them who was wearing a US Navy cap and sunglasses, with deep brown skin called back to them in his smooth voice and asked, "Are you sure you do not want to stay?" They hopped on the train.

Cleo saw the sun; it was like the world going down somewhere that she did not recognize. She felt grown, moved, and different. At Tanger, they got out and made their way back to the ticket office at the port. The window was closed. The boat was to leave in an hour. Chuck pushed and pushed, running around asking all kinds of people who spoke no English. The sun was going down. Cleo had read the timetables. There were no more boats after this. No one stirred on deck. Cleo heard the call to prayer, wailing beauty across the seething city. Finally, she headed up towards the entry to the boat as Chuck haggled around. The people at the boat finally opened the ticket window, but told them that no tickets were being sold. Cleo felt relieved for herself but worried for Chuck. Finally, he erupted in an accented Southern salvo, and they agreed to sell him a ticket. It was clear, and Cleo was glad that she had not gotten into more trouble. Thinking back about her Dad's autobiography, however, Cleo had just been home. The boat went back past Gibraltar again and Cleo was relieved, in a way, to see Spain. She got off on that continent and Chuck and she took the next train. She was really grimy. She also had not showered since Oslo. Finally, Chuck said that her feet 'really smelled'. Cleo was offended, but went and found a pay shower somewhere in some city.

Cleo was in Southern France. Bob had told her about Cap d'ai, on the Riviera. 'Why not?' she thought. Cleo met Debra again and they took the train and stopped in Monoco and got out. Bob had told her about the casino she went into in Monte Carlo at fourteen. 'A tough life,' Cleo thought. She saw the casinos, but did not go in. She viewed the amazing cars rolling by and watched the sun play on the water. They got back on the train to Cap d'ai. This small place seemed isolated from the other towns. Cleo walked down the amazing rock steps onto the beach, looking at the boats in the harbor. The beach was rock, and different than any beach Cleo had ever seen. She had wine and bread and looked out on a view that Bob had seen at fourteen. She took the train again, heading for Brittany, to find a small town Bob had crepes in when he was there. To go hundreds of miles for a crepe, that was Cleo. But she wanted to do what he had done, while she was still young. The night train was rhythmically winding through France, the wine and bread lulling her into utter joy. She listened to French radio, the sound soothing her. The song was unmistakable.

'And behold a mighty city
Broken in the dust again
Oh God, pride of man
Broken in the dust again'

The song played once; then again. The French announcer was saying again and again "Cipollina...Cipollina". Cleo understood. John Cipollina was dead. She had just seen him, so out of it that they had to prop him up on the WOW Hall stage. The sad song filled the small train compartment. Others nodded and talked in French about it. Cleo cried, not because she knew him or that he was the most famous musician, but this was it, the 60s were gone; the San Francisco sound, all the fun at the Saloon and in Golden Gate Park. Done. Finé. Cleo wrote a poem about Cipollina; something that she had just started doing. The music was everywhere. She was heading to Plouescat with her heart laden with sadness for the abuse victims like Gamble, the ill like Bob, the junkies like Nargo, the protesters who never got justice, the old man in Morocco, ladling every night, the tethered monkeys in the Tanger square. It was all so vast to her then, unlike now.

Cleo would not feel it anymore the same way. It would go

down a darker path of swollen livers and cancerous colons. Life was constricted no matter how far flung she went. The banks and the users would be around every corner. Cleo had worked so hard for what she had, and people wanted parts of it, all of it. Tattered clothes wouldn't keep them away. The tower of speakers with horns on top and the pictures of Cipollina in the Rock and Roll Hall of Fame could not replace him and his time period. The ties that hold people down and the need to bow down when you want to scream would take over. Cleo didn't believe in the unsullied beauty anymore. It was there in Morocco and France and in Atlanta with the LeBlancs. The beauty had been stolen, and Cleo had no insurance. It is gone, 'broken in the dust again.'

Brittany, Bretagne, was a different France. The artichoke fields spread before her; the farms and the cows and the old trucks. The train went to Brest, and Cleo looked on the map for Plouescat. Cleo asked, in limited French, where the bus was. They told her it did not go all the way to the town. Cleo was the only outsider, walking to the bus stop and putting her coins into the old box on the rickety bus. People smiled at her. She took the bus through the artichoke fields and got off. She saw the road sign, small and thin, with the kilometers written on its face. Cleo walked out onto the road and put her thumb out. The little cars motored by as in a Tatti film. Cleo expected to see the naughty schoolchildren in uniform as well, in black and white. A small, black car pulled over and a middle-aged Frenchman gestured.

"Plouescat?" Cleo asked.

"*Oui*," he replied and they were off. His accent was a bit different, and they jumbled through conversations. The road intersections were small, with four way stop signs. Cleo saw dust and farms and an open sky. The driver smiled when he dropped Cleo off in the tiny town. There was a small post office and a few shops. The rock buildings seemed ancient. Cleo saw a building with a kitchen. She walked in and the farmer people smiled. Their clothing were a bit dirty from the fields, but impeccably tailored. Cleo looked at the menu, and at the flowers outside the door. She ordered what she had come 10,000 miles for. She had a crepe so fluffy that it dissolved on her tongue as ambrosia. She drank red wine and watched the people walk by, sitting in chairs, smoking and talking. Cleo thought of Bob, and how he sometimes bought Dunhills, and Gitanes too if he ever found them. She got up and walked to the edge of town, the afternoon sun radiating out on her as at the end of European movies.

This was the part of the country where the ships had come in during the Great War, supplying the soldiers with weapons, food, uniforms, and essentials. One could imagine truckloads of supplies and army men traversing the roads, with women peering out of the farmhouse windows as the caissons rolied by. Cleo put out her thumb and got a ride back to Brest, where she again took the train to the outside of Paris, where Ed, Debra, and she met up once more for the afternoon. Deb had purchased a new Euro flag to show to one of her professors. Cleo fingered her francs, and got on the train. She went through Paris again, going to the parks and the banks of the Seine. Before she headed to the Schiphol airport, she spent a night out, watching Europeans at the height of their wave of glory, spending and drinking and smoking. She had just enough for a tiny hunk of a 'gift', which she sent through the mail to Bob. Cleo gleefully bought the padded envelope, went outside, put her gift in a bit of coffee, and put it in the mail. She felt invincible.

+++